April's Desires

A Larry Macklin Mystery-Book 6

A. E. Howe

Books in the Larry Macklin Mystery Series:

November's Past (Book 1)

December's Secrets (Book 2)

January's Betrayal (Book 3)

February's Regrets (Book 4)

March's Luck (Book 5)

April's Desires (Book 6)

May's Danger (Book 7)

Copyright © 2017 A. E Howe

ISBN: 0-9862733-8-4
ISBN-13: 978-0-9862733-8-4

DEDICATION

For Melanie—Not only does she make these books
possible through her advice, editing and support, but she
also makes the effort worthwhile.

CHAPTER ONE

I was on call Sunday when dispatch sent me out to the crime scene that would ruin my day. A body had been found in the backyard of a house in one of the older and seedier parts of Calhoun.

It was a beautiful morning, pleasantly warm with just a hint of the summer heat to come. April is one of the best months in north Florida. I tried not to think about the gruesome scene that was waiting for me and rolled down the window, enjoying the moment.

Though I didn't know it yet, this would be far from an ordinary case—no drug deal gone bad, suicide, accident or overdose. Death is never good, but some cases are resolved quickly, easily and with a hefty dose of justice. Other investigations try the foundations of our system. This was going to be one of the latter.

The small wood-frame house was rundown, its yard more dirt than grass. A couple of older cars were parked haphazardly in the driveway and two Adams County Sheriff's patrol cars were lined up at the curb. I pulled in behind them. As I got out of my car, one of the deputies, a woman who'd joined the department a year before, came up to meet me.

"Hey, Sandy, what have we got?"

"Somebody went to town on this kid," she said, obviously shaken up by the scene.

I'd worked with Matti Sanderson a few times. She was tough and professional. Her solid 5'9" frame always looked comfortable wearing her uniform and equipment. Unlike some rookies, Sandy seemed a natural, so if she was shaken up then it must have been bad.

"Martel is watching over the body. We've got three people in the house. One of them, David Benson, called it in. I've been out here making sure that they don't leave and that no one else tries to enter. I hope you don't mind, but I went ahead and told dispatch that you're going to need the crime scene techs."

"Good job. Run some crime scene tape across the driveway and get someone else out here to help. If none of our deputies are available, see if you can get a trooper from the highway patrol or an officer from the Calhoun police." On Sunday mornings we usually ran a light detail. If there was an accident or another emergency, then we had to take help from wherever we could find it.

"When someone shows up, go inside and make sure that the witnesses are behaving. Keep them separate."

It was probably too late to keep them from talking to each other, but it was better to close the barn door after the cows were out than to never close the door at all. Or whatever.

I retrieved a pair of rubber gloves from the trunk of my car, put on protective booties and headed around to the back of the house. The side of the house was almost completely hidden by azaleas that hadn't been trimmed in a decade or more. I had to step around an old screen that had fallen from one of the windows, but I knew it wasn't a clue as it was half buried by leaves and dirt.

Deputy Andy Martel was standing near the screened-in back porch, looking at anything except the body of the young man that lay about ten feet from the steps of the porch. He was on his side in a fetal position, his hands raised as though to protect his head from the blows that had crushed his skull. I understood what had bothered Sandy. He looked like a child curled up, defenseless against the onslaught that had killed him.

"Have you found anything interesting?" I asked Martel.

"Nope."

He was the most laconic deputy I'd ever met. Most cops love to hear themselves talk, but not Martel. If you wanted information from him, you had to ask. Someone had told me it was because Martel's family was from northern Wisconsin. Something about those long winters, I guess.

"Do we have a name?"

"Todd Harper."

Todd? Something about the name and the body rang a bell. I bent down and gently lifted the elbow that was blocking most of his face, then backed away quickly, feeling dizzy. My mind froze as I tried to make sense of what I was seeing. Then it raced ahead, considering all the possible ramifications of this murder.

Of course the name had rung a bell. I had seen the young man just the afternoon before. I couldn't prevent my mind from replaying the events of Saturday.

I'd spent the morning in Tallahassee with my girlfriend, Cara Laursen. We'd strolled through the arts and crafts at the Downtown Marketplace in the city's chain of parks, then sat on the terrace at Harry's and enjoyed some of the best New Orleans-style food this side of the Crescent City. We were headed home when I remembered that Pete Henley, my old partner, had wanted me to come to his daughter's softball game that afternoon. Eager to keep the beautiful day going, I looked over at Cara.

"Would you like to go to a softball game?"

She gave me a funny look. "I didn't know that you were a fan."

"It's Pete's daughter. She's got a big game this afternoon.

Scouts coming and the whole bit."

"She a senior?"

"No, junior, but with a good game Pete says she might be able to lock up a scholarship. She's been contacted by a couple of schools already. And they're playing Leon High School today."

"She must be excited."

"I'm not sure who's more excited, her or Pete. With two daughters and the hope that they'll both go to college in the next few years, he's desperate for some financial help. Deputies don't exactly pull in the big bucks." I certainly knew that to be true. Even without kids, there were months that I felt like I had to scrape up the money for my bills.

"I'm game. Pun intended," Cara said, flashing a smile.

"You play any sports?" I asked naively.

"Are you kidding? You've met my parents. They both think that team sports are the stepping stones to conformity, which leads to the subjugation of the soul," she answered with a grin.

I should have known better. Cara's mom and dad were what I'd imagine you'd get if you dropped an Irish country girl and a Viking warrior down in the middle of a commune. In fact, they currently lived in a co-op down in Gainesville that was only a few steps removed from a commune.

We parked in the Adams County High School lot, where several cars and a couple of buses were taking up about half the spaces. We walked out to the softball field where dozens of people were milling about while another seventy-five people sat in the bleachers, watching the Leon High girls warming up on the field.

I saw Pete right away. At almost three hundred pounds, he was hard to miss. He was standing near the dugout, talking to his oldest daughter, Jenny, who was dressed in her uniform and trying not to look like she was talking to her dad. I spotted Pete's younger daughter, Kim, sitting in the stands with her mom, Sarah.

We walked over to Pete and Jenny, whose eyes lit up as

soon as she caught sight of me. I figured that she had been standing there looking for a way to escape her dad, and I was her salvation.

"Mr. Macklin. Wow! It's so cool you came," she said, interrupting her father and causing him to look around.

"Hey, Larry!" the big guy said, all smiles. "Cara, how are you?" he asked, pulling her into a big bear hug. He had recently given her a few shooting lessons out at the department's gun range and they had quickly formed a mutual admiration society.

"I was just telling Jenny to listen to Coach Terry. He's been after her all season to—"

"I've got it, Dad. Don't worry."

"And don't get nervous."

"You're the one that's nervous."

"I'm the one that's going to have to shell out the big bucks for college if you don't get a scholarship," he joked. Pete had one of the best relationships with his family of any deputy in the department. Even though my father was the sheriff, Pete was my model for how to do the job and have a home life that made the job worth doing.

"I've got this," Jenny said.

"She's the starting pitcher today," Pete said proudly.

Jenny blushed and rolled her eyes.

"I've got to go warm up."

"Hug for luck," Pete said, giving her a quick one before she turned and trotted through the gate onto the field.

We all went up into the stands to sit with Sarah and Kim. Sarah was one of the nicest people I'd ever met, with a dry sense of humor and eyes that were soft but deep. She reminded me of the folks that my grandmother had called "old souls." Granny would always say that they were too wise to have only lived once.

I found myself sitting between Kim and Cara. "Are you working on any murders?" Kim asked me.

She was fourteen and, to her father's blushing admiration, wanted to go into law enforcement. The young

9

lady had come out just a month earlier to help with a search for a missing person, and her observation of a group of vultures had led to the body being discovered inside a drainage pipe.

"Not right now. And I'm happy about that," I told her, smiling.

"Yeah, I can understand that."

"How are you doing?" I was worried that finding a dead body might have caused her some distress, but I avoided mentioning it directly in case I dredged up memories that she was trying to push down.

"Okay," she answered, then went on as though she had read between the lines of my question. "I had some nightmares after finding that body. But they're gone now."

"So have you changed your mind about being a cop?"

"No. When I told Mom about the bad dreams, she said that my imagination was probably worse than the reality."

Pete had kept her back so that she hadn't actually seen the bloated and decaying body inside the culvert, but having seen it myself I doubted that her mother was right.

"So she bought me a book called *Death's Acre* about the body farm they have up in Tennessee."

My eyebrows lifted.

Pete was sitting on the other side of Kim and had been listening in on our conversation. "I'm not sure you should be telling the whole world that we got you that book," he told her.

"You didn't want to," she said accusingly.

"Mother knows best, I guess," he responded.

"I don't have nightmares anymore," Kim the realist told him. "And I may want to be a pathologist." She turned back to me. "Did you know that, after the first twelve hours, insects and the different stages that they go through are the best way to tell when someone died?"

"I'm afraid that I did," I joked with her. Actually, it wasn't that much of a joke. I really did wish that I knew less about dead bodies and their decomposition.

"I think it's really interesting. Now I wish I could have seen that body," Kim said as much to her dad as to me.

"No, you don't," Pete said firmly. "When you become a pathologist you can look at all the corpses you want, but for right now you should be thinking about kid stuff."

"You take me out to the range," she responded. I'd seen her shoot and she wasn't bad.

"Hush," Pete said, looking around comically. "You're going to get your mother and me thrown in the poky for child abuse."

I noticed that several of the other folks sitting around us were trying to suppress smiles. Probably everyone in the stands knew Pete and his family.

Out on the field, practice was over. The two teams came out and lined up in front of their dugouts, and we all stood for the national anthem.

"Crap," I heard Pete mutter under his breath just after we sat back down. I looked over and saw him staring at a young man who'd just walked up to the fence next to the home team's dugout. Pete was shooting daggers at the back of the kid, who looked scruffy even from this distance.

The game went well for Jenny. She didn't allow any runs and only a few hits during the first seven innings. Whenever she returned to the dugout she would give the young man a slight wave and a quick look, but at one point I thought I also saw a frown cross her face. Several times I heard Pete actually growl, and Sarah would place her hand on his knee, restraining him as effectively as if she had wrapped both hands around him.

Jenny was finally taken out of the game and a relief pitcher put in. Adams County ended up losing, but it was clearly not because of Jenny's performance. With the game over, we all made our way down the bleachers. I could feel the stands rock with each step that Pete took. He was watching the young man, who was heading directly for the team as they came off of the field.

Jenny stopped outside the gate and said something to the

young man, who put his hand on her arm. She backed away from him, and he immediately stepped toward her again.

I was following Pete with Cara, Sarah and Kim trailing us. Pete was focused on Jenny and the man and I decided to stick close to him. This had the feel of a situation that could spiral out of control quickly.

The man put his hand on Jenny's arm again and this time she slapped it away. When that happened, Pete broke into a jog and I ran to catch him. Jenny saw her father coming and stepped between him and the young man.

"No!" she shouted. Behind Jenny, I saw a slight smile cross the man's lips.

"Get your hands off of her!" Pete said through clenched teeth as he continued to bull his way forward. At this point I managed to cut in front of him with only six feet to go before he'd be nose to nose with them. Pete pushed me another three feet as I tried to slow his momentum.

"Pete, cool down," I said, planting my feet and putting my hands against his chest.

"Get out of my way," he said, looking past me at the young man.

"Todd's leaving," Jenny said to Pete.

"He'd better be running," Pete said louder than was necessary. A small crowd of people was now watching our little tableau. I even saw a couple of phones pointed our way.

"Stop it!" I barked straight into Pete's face and, for the first time since this had started, I had his full attention.

"He grabbed her arm," he growled at me.

I had never seen Pete go full Papa Bear. His anger was truly impressive. I decided that I needed to focus a bit on the other half of the problem. "You need to get the hell out of here," I told Todd, who had only three feet, Jenny and me between him and an unpleasant evening at the hospital.

"No way. This is a public—" he started, but Jenny turned to him and put a stop to his suicidal declaration.

"Go home, Todd. I told you I don't want you here," she said, clearly frustrated with him.

"I want to see you again."

"Not now."

"Meet me later," he pleaded.

"Can't you understand, she doesn't want to see you," Pete said and started pushing forward again like a bulldozer.

"Maybe," Jenny said to Todd, clearly not wanting to, but eager to bring an end to this embarrassing situation.

"When?" Todd asked.

Pete growled.

"Later. Just go!"

"My house." And then he reached out, possessively running his hand up Jenny's waist toward her breast.

A batboy chose just that moment to stop within arm's reach of us with a duffle bag full of bats and Pete, quick as lightning, reached out and grabbed one of the bats. I saw it happen in that weird slow motion of accidents and made my decision. I lowered my hold on Pete and then pushed forward, taking him down using leverage. I had to clench my teeth and lock my arms around his legs to keep him from struggling free.

"I'll take care of you. Don't you come near my family again, you son of a bitch!" Pete raged. I heard the bat thump on the ground a couple of times as I clung on for dear life.

Anyone watching at that moment or seeing the video later would have thought that Pete was completely out of control. I knew differently. The man had a .45 caliber Glock 21 on his waist that he could have pulled at any time. He was the department's firearms instructor and was one of the fastest and best shots I'd ever met. Pete never made a move toward his gun. But that argument paled next to the frothing anger that everyone could see.

Holding onto Pete, I couldn't tell what was going on behind me, but Cara told me later that Todd took off as soon as Pete grabbed the bat. Jenny had looked mortified, and Sarah had taken her to their car as Pete tried to regain a measure of his composure—no small challenge with me wrapped around his legs.

"He's gone. You can let go of me," Pete said in a small voice. I turned my head to see the crowd beginning to disperse. Half of the audience looked embarrassed while the other half looked like they had enjoyed the show.

I helped Pete to his feet. The batboy was still standing there in shock. Pete, shamefaced, gave him back the bat. Two large men, one of whom I recognized as the coach, were standing behind us.

"Pete, I've got to report this," the coach said.

"Mr. Henley, I should tell you that I don't know if I can let you back on school property. We have very strict rules about fighting at school events," said the other man, who I later learned was the principal. "Especially adults."

"I'm sorry," Pete said lamely. "I'm..." He wanted to explain, but he had been on the other side too many times and knew that you can't explain your way out of a justified punishment. He just put up his hands and said, "You're right," then turned and started toward his car.

"Pete," I said, catching up with him. "Don't worry. I'll talk to Dad."

Pete and I both knew that videos were going to be circulated and that this was going to be a problem for the department. I would've never used the fact that my father was the sheriff for my own benefit—truth was, I probably couldn't—but I was more than willing to do anything I could to help Pete. If I had any influence with Dad, I'd use every bit of it to defend a man I knew to be one of our best.

"This is going to be a shit storm," Pete said morosely. "I saw the cameras."

"Maybe no one will post the video," I said, knowing that it was probably uploading to various platforms as we spoke.

"I hate that kid. Jenny tried to break it off with him a month ago, but he won't let go. Scares me." Pete stopped and looked me in the eye. "How many cases of assault, stalking, even murder, have started like this?" he asked.

"You aren't wrong. But you've put yourself in a position now where you can't go anywhere near him. Look, I'll help you with this any way I can. Right now, you need to go home and take care of Jenny. Don't worry about anything except making things right at home." I knew that a plea to his nesting instinct was the best way to get him focused on something productive.

"You're right." Pete looked toward his car where his wife and two daughters were talking. Jenny looked devastated as her mother comforted her.

After we left the school, I called Dad, explaining what had happened and warning him that there were going to be some PR issues over the incident. He thanked me for the heads-up while cursing social media.

CHAPTER TWO

It was hard to accept that Todd's body was lying on the ground in front of me barely twelve hours later. The same Todd that Pete had threatened, and who now looked like he'd been hit repeatedly with a blunt object to the head. Like a baseball bat. Not for one minute did I think that Pete killed him, but that in itself was a problem. As the lead investigator, I had to be able to evaluate all suspects without bias.

"Son of a bitch," I said.

"What's going on?"

I turned to see Clark Macon, one of our civilian crime scene techs, followed by one of the interns that had been working with the team for several months.

"Where's Shantel?" I asked, not worrying if I hurt Clark's feelings. He was a fine tech and I'd have been happy to have him if I was processing a burglary or an assault, but there was no way that he was going to be the primary crime scene tech on this case.

"She's at church. Not that she's even on call this weekend. And Marcus is out of town," Clark said, sounding a bit dejected. He was in his fifties with droopy eyelids, a receding hairline and a potbelly that got in the way whenever he tried to reach the ground. He'd been a 911 dispatcher for years, but the stress was killing him so he had been retrained and moved over to the evidence room.

I took out my phone and texted Shantel, asking her to call me and typing *911* in the message. She immediately called me back and I explained the situation.

Fifteen minutes later, Shantel Williams pulled up to the curb in her personal car. She was dressed to the nines for church, her dark skin complemented by the bright yellow dress she was wearing.

"Clark, I really appreciate you being here, bringing the van and all, but I want you to keep those size elevens away from the crime scene for now," she told him with the kindly smile one would give to a slow child.

"Whatever you say, Miss Shantel."

"Bring the video camera out. I'll film it first," she told him, then turned to me. "I'm sure glad I keep some sneakers in the car," she said, slipping blue booties on over her shoes and pulling on a pair of gloves. "Is it really as bad as you were saying?"

"Honestly, it's worse."

As Shantel walked back to the body, I took out my phone again and did something I should have done already. I called my current partner, Darlene Marks. She wasn't on duty, but this case was going to require that we back up our backup.

We'd only been working together for a couple of months and we still hadn't ironed out all of our differences, but we'd come to a place of mutual respect. When I called her, she had already seen the video of Pete's altercation with Todd posted on Facebook. I wasn't surprised. I had been born and raised in Adams County while Darlene had moved here a decade ago to take a job with the Calhoun Police Department, yet she seemed to know more people and have her ear to the ground better than I did. When I explained who the victim was and how he had died, Darlene didn't hesitate.

"On my way," she said and hung up.

While I waited for Darlene, I decided to go inside the house and meet the witnesses. The interior reminded me of my college days, smelling of neglect, transience and one too many parties. Sandy was dutifully standing guard, looking down a small dark hallway with two doors on each side and a window at the end. Beside her stood a thin young woman wearing black jeans and a white blouse and chewing on her fingernails.

"I had the other two witnesses stay in their rooms," Sandy told me. "This is Anna Davis. Her boyfriend is in the room farthest down on the right. The bathroom is across from his room. Todd lived in the first room on the right and the other kid is in the room across from his."

"Anna, I'm Deputy Larry Macklin. Can you tell me who discovered the body?" I figured it was safe to ask some basic questions before Darlene arrived since I had Sandy as a witness.

Before Anna answered me, she pulled her phone out of her pocket and looked at it. In that moment I realized that I was an idiot. I held up my hand to keep her from speaking and said, "First, we'll need to hold onto your phone."

"What for?" she protested.

"We can't let you talk to anyone for the moment." She looked like she was going to argue. "We'll give it back shortly." Grudgingly, she handed it over.

"I'll be right back. Sandy, will you get any phones from the other two roommates?"

I walked quickly outside. I'd screwed up by not getting their phones immediately, though they'd already had time to call or text friends and family between the time that the body was discovered and the first responders arrived. I wanted to get ahold of Dad so he could get a handle on things, including stopping Pete from doing anything stupid like rushing over here. In a small town, news always traveled fast. Now, thanks to smartphones, it traveled at the speed of light.

I caught Dad just as he was going into a church service on the south side of town. He was making it a point to spend every Sunday between now and the fall election at one of the hundred-plus churches in the county. I briefed him and listened to him cuss for a couple of minutes. I hoped he wasn't too close to the church.

"I'm glad you've called in Marks and Shantel. I'm going to call FDLE and see if they'll send someone. We'll need to cover all the bases for Pete and there can't be any appearance that we're covering anything up. I'll call Pete and fill him in. We'll have to have a review of his behavior at the school at the very least. For right now, I'm going to suspend him with pay." There was more cussing. "I'm going to want a briefing from you and Marks this afternoon. Maybe we'll get lucky and this won't have anything to do with the altercation Pete had with this kid."

As I was hanging up, I saw Darlene arrive. I also noticed that a few of the neighbors were watching us from their yards. *We'll get to you*, I thought.

Darlene walked up to the house and looked at me for a moment as though she was trying to make up her mind about something. Finally she said, "I want to be clear. I saw the video, and I know that you and Pete are solid friends. Personally, I respect Pete. He's the best firearms instructor I've ever had, and I've worked alongside him and have always been impressed with his skills as an investigator. But—and this is a big but—he's a suspect now just the same as anyone else. Right now, I'm here to investigate this murder. If I think for one moment that you're obstructing the investigation in order to help Pete, I will go to our supervisors. If I think that they are perverting justice, I will go to the Florida Department of Law Enforcement or the State Attorney or both and file a complaint." She paused, still looking me square in the eye. "I know that's a mouthful, but I needed to lay my cards on the table."

"Fair enough. Let's go talk to the witnesses," I said, hoping that I could be fair and honest. But at this point I couldn't be sure. Actually, it would help knowing that Darlene was looking over my shoulder.

We decided to start with the man who had found the body. David Benson was Anna's boyfriend. He was sitting on his bed, staring at the floor. The room was decorated with stage show playbills and dust, and his clothes were scattered about the room. David wasn't going to win any Martha Stewart awards.

"You live here?" I started off after finding out that he was twenty-three years old, born in Tampa and working on a masters in theatre at Florida State University.

"We rent it."

"By 'we,' you mean you, Todd and…?"

"Dereck. Dereck Granger. Actually, Dereck's is the only name on the lease. So I guess, technically, he rents the house and we sublet from him. My dad's in real estate. The landlord is okay with it."

"How long have you all known each other?"

"I've known Dereck since high school, but I've only been living here since December. I'm taking a semester off and working with the Grove Theatre," he said, mentioning a small musical theatre in Calhoun. "Todd moved in about the same time."

"Tell us about finding the body."

"Nothing really to tell. I went out back," he looked at his watch, "about an hour ago, and there he was."

"Why did you go outside?" Darlene asked.

David rolled his eyes. "You know." Darlene and I just looked at him. "Look, Anna takes forever in the bathroom in the morning. We only have the one, so I stepped outside to take a piss." He looked genuinely embarrassed by this admission.

"Did you piss first or see the body right away?" Darlene forged ahead, refusing to recognize the man's embarrassment.

"I stepped out, started to… piss and when I got… going, I looked around and saw him."

"You knew he was dead?"

"Oh, yeah. Wasn't any doubt about that. I got my jeans

all wet putting myself back in and ran inside and woke up Dereck. It really freaked the shit out of me. Dereck had to tell me to call 911. Like, my mind was gone." He sounded like the experience had really shaken him, but he was a theatre major, so it could have been just an act.

"How did everyone in the house get along?" I asked.

"Okay," he said unconvincingly.

"I'll tell you how this works," I said in a brotherly way. "We're going to ask everyone these same questions. Not just the other two people currently in the house, but everyone we can get ahold of. Neighbors, friends, co-workers, you name it. Whenever we get conflicting answers, our radar is going to start to ping, and that's going to cause us to take a hard look at the people giving us different answers. Why? Because we'll know that one of them is lying to us. Now, I'm going to ask one more time. Were there any interpersonal conflicts between the people in the house?"

"Just stupid stuff. Nothing that led to... this."

"Every detail is important when someone gets murdered."

He flinched when I said the word *murdered*. "None of us really liked Todd," he said, almost in a whisper. "Maybe Dereck did."

"Why not?" I asked, but I could imagine the answer, having seen the guy in action the night before.

"He just... was an... ass. You know?"

"You need to give me some specifics," I prodded.

"Stupid stuff. He ate whatever was here, no matter whose food it was. You had to beg him for his share of the rent and utility money. Anna thought he was hitting on her a couple of times. Just crap like that."

"Did you think he was hitting on Anna?" Darlene jumped in.

"Nothing like that. Hey, no!" David's eyes got big. I could tell that he was realizing for the first time that he could be a suspect in Todd's murder.

"Did you?"

"She's a good-looking woman. A lot of guys look at her. I never worried about it. I'm not the super-jealous type."

Maybe, maybe not, I thought. "When was the last time that you saw Todd alive?"

"When Anna and I went to my room last night. This room. I guess about midnight. Like I said, she didn't really like hanging around him very much. When we came in here, Dereck and Todd were still… I don't know when they went to bed." David was horrible at keeping secrets.

"What were they doing? Drugs? Look, I'm not interested in anything that doesn't directly link back to this murder." I thought about telling him that if any drugs were found in the common areas of the house, then he was already screwed. The house was going to be thoroughly searched, and anything that was hidden would be found. But I didn't want to make him any more paranoid. It might just push him to lawyer up.

"You need to give me a timeline for what you and, as far as you know, your roommates did last night."

"Nothing. Todd got home about eight, I guess. He was all pumped up about what had happened at the softball game. Anna wanted us to go somewhere, but I didn't want to because I don't get paid until next Friday, so I'm, like, broke. At some point, Todd talked Dereck into getting food from Express Burgers."

"They went and got the food?"

"Yeah, and brought it back. Dereck even brought me a burger. By the time they got back, Todd was showing all of us that video of the cop going berserk. After that, we all watched a movie, then Anna and I came in here."

"What movie did you watch?" Asking for details was one of the best ways to trip up a liar.

"Some dumb film about the future and time travel. It had Tom Cruise. Not my thing."

"But you watched it anyway?"

"Like I said, I didn't have money to go out, and Dereck wanted to watch it. He's really into sci-fi."

"And Dereck and Todd stayed up?"

"We could hear them watching another movie."

"When did you fall asleep?"

"I guess it was a little after midnight. I was supposed to go to work this morning. Hey, can I have my phone back?"

"Not until we're done questioning all of you."

"Did you take Anna's phone away too?"

"Yep."

"I'd like to see that. I can't ever get her to put her phone down."

I marveled at how he could think of something so trivial when his roommate's body was curled up in the backyard with its head bashed in. Was I so self-centered at his age?

After a few more basic questions, we left David and moved on to Anna. We had just walked up to her when my phone vibrated. *Why doesn't someone take my phone away?* I thought. Caller ID said it was Dad, so I excused myself and went out on the porch.

"I've broken the news to Pete and told him to stay at home. What's your status?"

I gave him a quick rundown of everything that had happened since we last spoke.

"Okay, finish up the interviews with the three witnesses at the house, but as soon as you're done with them, I want you and Marks in my office. We need to talk about how we're going to proceed."

"Yes, sir," I responded and went back in the house.

Anna's account followed David's story pretty closely. She remembered that the movie had been *Edge of Tomorrow* and added that she liked Tom Cruise.

"What was your relationship with Todd like?"

"Yuck! I didn't have a relationship with him. He was a pig. I couldn't believe that he was stalking some seventeen-year-old. Maybe it wasn't illegal, but it was sleazy. Really, everything he did was creepy. I wanted David to move out of here because of him, but Dereck and David are, like, friends from high school. And Dereck is really nice. So…"

She was fidgeting and, every once in a while, would touch her pocket, missing her phone.

"How did Dereck and Todd get along?"

"Dereck gets along with everybody, but he's been trying to get Todd to move out. Todd is... was, I guess... He never paid his bills. He sponged off everyone. Tried to hitch rides with me. He wanted more than a car ride. Eck!" After a moment she added, "I guess I shouldn't talk bad about him. Don't get me wrong, none of us would have hurt him."

We interviewed Dereck in his room. He looked uncomfortable and lost.

"We just need to ask you a few questions," I told him.

Dereck's room was exceptionally neat. I noticed a large black garbage bag that looked about to burst open sitting behind the door. While he was waiting, had he cleaned up anything that he didn't want us to see?

"I don't understand. Someone killed him? That's crazy." Dereck was, hands-down, the most shaken up of the witnesses. He gave us his version of the evening, which varied more by degrees than anything else. He did make a point of mentioning how ticked off Anna was at Todd.

"She did *not* like him. No, sir. Really thought he was being rapey when he talked about that girl in the video. Todd could be a real ass, but he also knew how to have fun. Anna just wasn't in the mood for his bullshit. I think she and David may have been having some issues. Don't know. Don't stick my nose where it doesn't belong."

"You got along with Todd? Even though he didn't pay his bills?" I asked.

"You know, it's all good. He'd come up with the money when I had to have it. That's how he was. Always pushing things as far as he could. Todd would get people pissed off and then back off right before it went crazy."

"You don't think he meant to make the cop in the video mad?"

"Oh, now that's a different story. He really had the hots for that girl. He'd get on the scent and you could hardly hold him back." Dereck looked up at Darlene and shrugged.

"You ever see him cross the line with a woman?" Darlene asked him.

"What do you mean?"

"I mean touch someone who didn't want to be touched. I mean keep going when a woman told him to stop. That's what I mean."

"No, I've never seen him go too far." Dereck sounded hesitant.

"But you think he could have?" I pushed.

"Definitely possible."

"Is there anyone you can think of that might have wanted to hurt him?"

"Not like… dead," he said emphatically.

"But other ways?"

"Like I've been sayin', Todd got under people's skin."

"We'll want a list of all the people whose skin he got under. Beside their names, put what he did to piss them off."

"Hey, man, I can't be doing that. Rattin' people out."

"We'll be back later this afternoon. Have the list ready for us by then," I said, ignoring his protest. "You've already said that there are quite a few people, so we'll want to see that reflected in the list."

We left the unhappy man with a pen and a blank sheet of paper.

"Your thoughts?" I asked Darlene as we walked to our cars.

"I don't see those three being involved. Not enough focus. The amount of anger and the disregard for the body—leaving it lying out in the open. Our killer is someone who's pretty callous. Of course, I'll be curious what the background checks on the three of them reveal. We find out one of them was involved in arson or had anger issues when they were younger, then that would be a whole 'nother can of worms."

"Agreed on all fronts. Finding the weapon would be helpful." Helpful was an understatement. The murder weapon is usually second only to the body in importance to an investigation.

"Dr. Darzi will probably be able to tell us what kind of weapon we're looking for," Darlene said, seeing our coroner's assistants arrive to take the body to the morgue. Word was that Darzi was at a conference in Orlando and wouldn't be back until tonight. I really wished we could have had the A Team on the scene.

CHAPTER THREE

The sheriff's office was deserted except for a few patrol deputies using the open desks to do paperwork. We found Dad in his office. As always, I did a quick scan for Mauser, his spoiled two-and-half-year-old Great Dane, but he was nowhere in sight.

"Jamie came over to watch him," Dad said. "I don't know what I'm going to do if that kid ever moves away. He and Mauser have really hit it off." I was pretty sure that it was because, like a child, Mauser appreciated someone who gave him some boundaries. Dad certainly never did.

As we sat down across from him, Dad addressed Darlene first. "You are going to be the lead on this investigation."

As I started to protest, he held up a hand to stop me. "I have a couple of choices here. One, I can turn the whole investigation over to FDLE. Two, I can call them in for assistance. Three, we can simply investigate it like we would any other case."

I started to open my mouth and got more hand, as well as the full power of Ted Macklin's quelling green-eyed stare. "I've decided on the middle option. It wouldn't be fair to Pete for us to investigate it like any other case. No matter how well we cleared him, there would always be someone who would suggest that we showed favoritism. I'm also not ready to turn the whole thing over to FDLE. They're good, but it wouldn't be their highest priority. This way, we'll keep control over the case and we'll make sure that no one can claim we're hiding anything. Which is why you can't be the lead. You're too close to Pete."

As much as I wanted to remain in charge of the investigation, I knew he was right to turn it over to someone who had the least ties to Pete who, for now, would have to be considered the prime person of interest.

"What's Pete's status?" Darlene asked.

"Suspended with pay, based on the incident at the school. He's just a person of interest in the murder case until you tell me something different. I'll get Major Parks to do an internal affairs review of his behavior, but, honestly, looking at the video I didn't see anything that would rise above the level of bad judgment. But I do want to get statements on the record from witnesses concerning Todd's behavior toward Pete's daughter. Assuming that what you told me is true, there isn't a person in this county that would question Pete's reaction."

In Adams County, folks considered defending your daughter justification for almost anything, up to and including murder. Unfortunately, the video didn't show what Todd had done to Jenny. Not that that alone would have justified murder, but if Pete had slugged Todd for it, it would have been next to impossible to seat a jury that would have convicted him.

"I'll need to interview Pete and, depending on the interview, I might go for a search warrant," Darlene said, making me cringe.

I wondered how Pete would react to an interview. The standard advice is that you shouldn't talk to law enforcement, period, and certainly not without a lawyer present. Too often an innocent person has said something out of naiveté during an interview that put them unjustly under an investigative microscope.

"Interview him, and if you can justify a search warrant,

do it and execute it," Dad said. He was going to do this the only way he could right now, by aiming straight at Pete.

As we were walking down the hall toward the front door, Darlene asked, "Do you want to call Pete about the interview, or do you want me to?"

"I'd prefer you did. I'm not sure if I could keep from telling him not to do it."

"Understood." She made the call and Pete foolishly agreed to let us come over.

Pete's house was a rambling ranch-style affair in a family neighborhood of mostly starter homes. Pete and Sarah had bought the home as newlyweds and loved the neighborhood so much that, instead of buying a larger home in a different area, they had just added onto their first home, leaving it looking a bit too large and ungainly. But, like Pete, it came across as friendly and welcoming.

I knocked on the front door. The garage was open and, if this had been a normal friendly visit, I would have walked into the garage and knocked on the door that I knew led into the kitchen. But there was nothing normal about this visit.

Pete opened the door, looking shell-shocked. His hair was uncombed and he was wearing an extra-large salmon-colored polo, khaki shorts and sandals. "Come on in," he said.

I could hear someone cooking in the kitchen as Pete led us into the living room. It had the neat, staged appearance of a place that was seldom used. I knew that the Henleys spent most of their time in the kitchen and the family room. Like a lot of folks in the South, they reserved the living room for formal occasions and unexpected guests.

"I can't believe any of this." Pete started talking before we could even sit down. "Yesterday was all my fault."

I wanted to tell Pete to stop. I knew that he meant the scene at the ballfield with Todd, but someone else might have interpreted a statement like that very differently.

"I shouldn't have lost my temper. And, of course,

everyone has a damn camera with them these days. Jenny's been freaking out about how many views the thing has gotten and the comments that people are making. And now the murder... I just don't understand the murder. What are the odds?"

"Pete, I've got to ask you all of the standard questions. You understand that, right?" Darlene said in a kindly voice. Was she really trying to be gentle with him, or was this just the standard get-the-suspect-to-trust-you routine?

"I understand. I also know that I would advise a friend not to give you an interview without advice from a lawyer. But I can't stonewall you. I just have to believe that things will work out." Pete's eyes had a faraway look, as though he was trying to see a future where everything was back to normal.

"After the game, what did you do?" Darlene had taken out a recorder and set it on the coffee table after asking Pete if it was okay.

"We came home. Jenny was very upset. She kept yelling at me."

"What in particular was it that upset her?"

Pete gave Darlene an exasperated look. "She's a teenage girl. Anything that draws attention to her has to be bad. Jenny hates a scene, and she thought that I had overreacted." He paused for a moment before adding, "I guess she was right."

"How did she feel toward Todd?"

"She thought that she could handle him. Jenny had told him that they were done weeks ago, but he wouldn't stop coming around. I told her again and again that she needed to be firm and cut him off."

"She didn't take your advice?"

"She admitted to me that she'd texted him back, and even taken his phone calls a couple of times."

"His behavior really worried you?" Darlene asked, and I knew how tricky the answer to this question could be.

Pete looked at the recorder before answering. "I've dealt

with domestic abuse. I know the signs. He was controlling and manipulative. So, yes, I was worried."

"Okay, Pete, I know you. You're a deputy, a man of action. I can't believe that you would allow your daughter to be in danger. So what did you do?"

"Ha, with my daughter involved I would have been safer dancing in a minefield. I was still trying to work it out. I wanted her to see the problem and take charge. I'm not an idiot. If I stepped in too early, I stood the risk of making the situation worse."

"But something set you off yesterday."

"Yes. I overreacted, I guess. He put his hand... He was taking liberties. I saw her tell him no and still he put his hand... He did it again."

"What exactly did he do?" Darlene pressed.

"He put his hand under... Actually, on the lower part of her breast." We watched as the anger Pete had felt yesterday resurfaced. His eyes blazed and his cheeks turned red as the words came out through clenched teeth. I was glad that we weren't recording video of the interview.

"And what did you do?" Darlene paused. "And we aren't specifically investigating what happened at the field. An internal affairs investigation is going to look into your behavior at the game and decide if any disciplinary action is called for." Darlene rattled this off in a professional tone of voice.

Pete frowned and I knew that the big guy was beating himself up over losing his cool. Now he had part of his family upset at him, the community was going to be scrutinizing his behavior and he'd risked his professional reputation. I remembered the self-recriminations he had suffered several years ago when he'd been through another internal affairs investigation because he had turned down his radio during a meal break and had failed to come to the aid of another deputy. Pete took his own failings very hard.

He looked at me and I shook my head *no*. I had sat back on the couch, hoping that I was out of Darlene's line of sight. Apparently I wasn't. She looked at me and sighed.

"And since it is subject to another investigation, we'll understand if you want to keep your answers regarding this incident brief and to the point."

"Naturally, I was upset, but several people persuaded me to calm down," Pete said very carefully. That was a much better answer than saying, "One of the deputies sitting in this room managed to restrain me from killing the son of a bitch."

"What did you do after that?"

"Everyone—by everyone I mean me, my wife and two daughters—was upset, so we agreed to go home. Originally we'd planned on driving into Tallahassee for dinner. But after the... incident, we all just wanted to get home. Jenny went to her room and stayed there the rest of the evening, except to come out on occasion and tell me how many views the video had gotten and to let me know that I had ruined her life. Sarah made dinner for the rest of us. Then Sarah, Kim and I watched TV until Kim went to her room to work on a school project. Sarah and I discussed the... Well, we talked until she went to bed about ten-thirty. I stayed up until midnight working in the garage and then went to bed. I didn't wake up until nine this morning."

"So from midnight to nine this morning, only your wife can vouch for your whereabouts?"

"That's true."

"And she was asleep most of that time?"

"Again true."

I wanted to go on record and say that this was the alibi of an innocent man, but I kept my mouth shut.

"Would your neighbors notice if you drove out in the middle of the night?" I asked. Pete often complained about one of his neighbors who couldn't keep his nose out of everyone's business.

"They would probably notice. Sam Branson would. He thinks he's a one-man neighborhood watch. I know in the past he's complained if one of us came home late. Or if I get a call out in the middle of the night," Pete confirmed.

I felt good getting that on record.

"We'll talk with him. Please don't contact him until we've had a chance to interview him."

"I won't," Pete said, knowing that any suspicion that he was tampering with a witness wouldn't go down well at all.

"Can we look around the house?" Darlene asked.

It was a routine question, but how was Pete going to take it? I could tell that he was thinking long and hard about it. He knew that we would be looking specifically for any shoes and clothes that he might have worn last night and, of course, for any object that might have been used to kill Todd.

Pete bit his lip and looked up at the ceiling. "Okay," he finally answered.

Darlene held up her phone. "Do you mind if I record as we walk through the house?"

"In for a penny, in for a pound," Pete said and nodded.

"Could you give a yes or no for the recording?" Darlene said and added, "Sorry."

"Yes, you can film your walk-through," Pete enunciated.

We went into the kitchen first, where Sarah was standing at the counter.

"Hi, Larry," she said to me. "I'm not sure we've met. I'm Sarah," she said to Darlene, who was filming the kitchen.

Darlene looked uncomfortable as she introduced herself.

"Pete's had good things to say about you. I'm glad you're investigating this... mess." Sarah's naturally optimistic nature was clearly being tried by the circumstances.

"We're going to do our best to find the guilty party," Darlene said, concentrating on the kitchen. She opened cabinets and the pantry while I scanned the room. I was trying to find anything that might have been used to kill Todd because I was sure that Pete was innocent. Any object we could find and test with a negative result would help Pete, not hurt him.

After we'd finish with all of the public areas, we started

on the bedrooms. With a deep sigh, Pete knocked on Jenny's door.

"What?" came the reply from the other side of the door.

"Larry and another investigator are here and need to look in your room," Pete said to the door.

After a short pause, the door opened. Jenny looked confused.

"I don't understand any of this. Did someone really kill Todd?" she asked, looking directly at me.

"I'm afraid it's true."

"That's insane." From her red eyes and the color in her cheeks, it wasn't a stretch to say that she'd been crying. Was she grieving for Todd? Or was it a more self-centered grief because her life was being turned upside down?

"Why do you want to look in my room?"

"They're going to want to ask you a few questions too," Pete said softly.

"I didn't do anything."

"We don't suspect you of anything," Darlene reassured her.

Jenny's eyes grew large, "Oh my God, you don't think Dad had anything to do with this? That's insane. Mr. Macklin, you can't think that. You know Dad."

I really wanted to tell her that I knew her father was innocent, but the video was running and that's all anyone would need to hear—one of the investigators on a case claiming that he knew a suspect was innocent before the investigation had even gotten started.

"We're going to find the person who did this. But right now we have to check out all of the people who interacted with Todd in the last twenty-four hours," I finally said, threading the needle with my answer.

She stepped out into the hall without another word. Pete put his hand on her shoulder and she allowed him to comfort her.

There were at least half a dozen softball bats in the room. It was my turn to sigh. Darlene filmed the tidy little room that was decorated with lots of pictures of athletes mixed with a number of feminine touches.

"Pete," Darlene called out to him, "it would help us out if we could take these bats in to be checked."

He poked his head into the room and I could see him agonizing over the decision. If he was innocent, then what harm could it do to let us take the bats in to be tested? But he also knew that labs made mistakes. If they misidentified blood on one of the bats, then all hell would break loose. And the reverse side of the coin ran the risk of making it look like he wasn't cooperating with the investigation.

"May as well take them. If it turns out that a bat was used, you'd just come back and get them with a search warrant," he finally said.

I turned to Jenny before we left her room. "Yesterday you told Todd that you might meet him at his house. Did you?"

"Nooooo. I just said that to get him to leave."

"Did you phone or text him?"

"No. He did text me a couple of times. And I think he tried calling me. I got a couple calls from numbers I didn't recognize. That was a trick he used sometimes when I was trying to break it off. He'd buy one of those prepaid phones or he'd borrow someone else's phone, trying to get me to answer. But last night I turned off the ringer and ignored all the calls."

"Can we see your phone?" Darlene asked.

Jenny looked at her dad. Pete nodded and Jenny handed her phone to Darlene. She scrolled through the texts and the missed calls, then handed the phone back to Jenny.

The search of the rest of the house was pretty routine. The garage was filled with Pete's ammunition reloading equipment and a huge safe bolted to the floor that held an impressive array of weapons, making me really glad that Todd hadn't been shot.

Finished with the inside of the house, we circled the outside and filmed the backyard and collected some tools from a shed so they could be examined. The backyard was mostly open with a wooded lot behind it.

"Does that lead over to the other street?" Darlene asked while filming.

"It does. They started to build over there during the housing boom in the nineties, but stopped when the economy went bust. There are several empty houses over on that street that have never sold."

I could see a couple of trails leading off into the woods. Pete saw me looking at them.

"Deer, raccoons and kids. Kim has a friend who lives on that street and they cut through a lot. We had a privacy fence up when we first moved here, but it rotted out and then Kim's friend moved in. I know I should put the fence back up, but..." The cobbler's son's shoes always have holes in them and the deputy doesn't take the proper security measures.

"Do you have security cameras?"

"No. There is a security light by the garage in front. And I've run bolts through the side of the garage door, so it's quite the operation to raise it. I did that when I turned it into my reloading and gun storage area."

Once we were finished and the camera and recorder were turned off, I apologized to Sarah and Pete and assured them that I knew he was innocent. Darlene didn't contradict me, and she didn't even give me a hard time about it after we left.

CHAPTER FOUR

We headed back to the crime scene, only to discover a couple of vans from two local news stations in Tallahassee waiting for us.

"You should go over and talk with them," I told Darlene, pointing at the news vans. A couple of cameramen were already filming the front of the house.

"Shouldn't it be the sheriff?" she asked and, for the first time, I heard hesitation in her voice. Had I found her weak spot? Was Darlene camera-shy?

"He always encourages investigators to step up and talk to reporters. Carefully, of course. Just the facts, ma'am."

"I don't know. Maybe you could?"

Inside, I was smiling. I shouldn't have enjoyed her discomfort, but I had never seen her show any fear of anything before. It was kind of nice to find out that she was human after all.

"I can't. I'm not the lead investigator, and I'm not the best person to be the face of this investigation because of my friendship with one of the suspects," I told her.

"I guess I could call the sheriff and see what he thinks."

"He's going to tell you to talk to them. His philosophy when it comes to news people is that if they can't talk to us, then they'll find someone else to talk to. Better they get the story directly from us."

Darlene was actually squirming in her seat. The thought of being on camera really made her nervous. She looked at me with pleading eyes.

"Look, it's simple. They don't expect you to be smooth and charming. All they want is an official statement. Take out a pad, write down the facts and stick to those. When they ask anything else, just tell them that the investigation is ongoing and that we'll provide updates when we can. That's Dad's canned phrase."

Darlene grabbed a pen and made a few notes.

"The reporters won't mind if you read it right off the pad. I've done it a couple of times when I was worried about going off script," I told her as she finished writing up her CliffsNotes.

"Okay, thanks," Darlene said nervously, fumbling the door handle as she got out.

I watched from a distance as she introduced herself to the news teams. She managed to pull herself together and looked like what she was—a sheriff's investigator who wasn't used to talking in front of a camera.

"You did great," I told her when she came back over to where I was standing.

"I guess." She watched them do a couple more reporter-on-scene shots before they packed up and left.

"See, all they wanted was an official statement. Now you can tell all your friends to watch you on the six o'clock news."

"God forbid."

We saw Shantel coming around the side of the house carrying a box filled with plastic evidence bags.

"They took the body a little while ago. I kept an eye on them. Wasn't Dr. Darzi, but they looked like they knew what they were doing. Darzi will be back tonight and will probably do the autopsy tomorrow. Late afternoon, most likely," Shantel said as she took the box and put it in the crime scene van. "One thing I did notice. His fly was unzipped. Not that that's the kind of thing I look for. Just thought you might find it interesting."

I thought about David going out in the backyard to urinate. Was that what Todd was doing?

"Find any smoking guns?" I asked her.

"Nothing that jumps out. That yard had a lot of junk in it. Cigarette butts, bottle caps, some beer cans under the bushes. Also found a pair of panties and a used condom. Most of it looked like it was more than a day old. But I'm not going to make those decisions out here in the field."

That was one of the qualities that made Shantel such a great tech. She wasn't going to leave evidence behind just because she thought it wasn't important. She'd do the work to bag it all up and let it be determined later if it might mean something. For all we knew, we might find out next week that an event that took place in the backyard a month ago had some bearing on this case. It was best to collect everything you could as soon as you could.

"If you have the time, let's go in and film his room," Darlene said to Shantel.

"Let me grab my camera." She rummaged around and brought out a small camera bag that contained a high-quality still camera, a video camera and supplies such as a small light, a ruler for perspective and extra batteries. "You all know that Pete had nothing to do with this, right?" she said as we followed her into the house.

The doorknob had been dusted for prints and was still covered in black dust. I opened it for Shantel, who methodically went around filming all the items in the room.

The room was roughly the same size as David's. Todd didn't have many possessions. A couple of large gym bags lay open on the floor. These were apparently what he had used for suitcases. While there was a shirt and pair of pants lying over the bed's footboard, most of his clothes were in the bags.

"Ready to go at a moment's notice," Darlene observed.

"I'm thinking he was someone who was used to being kicked out," I said.

Sitting on the floor beside the bed was a cell phone, an investigative gold mine. These days many cases are solved by messages and texts on cell phones. Darlene and I had to restrain ourselves from reaching down and picking it up. Shantel still had to photograph it, and then she'd need to process it for prints and DNA.

We all jumped when the phone started ringing. I squinted to read the caller ID, which said "Hex." *Interesting name*, I thought. I pulled out my phone, snapped a picture of the screen and then called the number.

"Hex, for whatever you desire," said the woman who answered.

"Hi, I'm a friend of Todd's."

"Nice, baby, what can I do for you?" she said, which didn't clue me in too much, though I thought I had a good idea where this was going.

"Todd said you were good," I said noncommittally.

"Baby, I'm the best. Just tell me what, where and when."

"How much?"

"You got to work that all out with Todd." She hesitated for a moment, then asked, "Are you with him now?"

"No."

"Oh, okay. I might need a ride. There'll be a discount if you pick me up."

"Let me talk price with Todd and I'll get back with you."

"Sure, baby. And… would you have Todd call me? Thanks, sweetie."

Shantel and Darlene were both staring at me.

"Seems Todd was running a woman named Hex."

"Haven't heard of her," Darlene said.

"Me neither. I'll talk to some of the guys working vice."

"I think this prick's murder is going to have a large pool of suspects. Good news for Pete," Darlene said.

"Not if we can't get to the bottom of it soon and find the one who actually knocked Todd on the head. As long as the murder remains unsolved, with that stupid video out there a lot of folks are going to be sure that Pete's the killer."

With so few personal possessions, it didn't take long to process the room. We didn't find anything else of much interest. There were some drugs in recreational amounts and his wallet, which had about a hundred dollars in it.

"Car next," Shantel said. I felt sorry for her having to supervise all the evidence collection by herself. Normally Marcus Brown would have handled half of it. But I was glad that she was here and that she wasn't leaving it to the second string.

Inside the car we found some trash and a little bit of drug residue, again in recreational amounts. The car had a perfumey smell, no doubt related to the transportation of Hex and any other ladies that he helped drive to facilitate their business endeavors.

At first I hadn't thought about the implications of Todd's business to Pete's predicament. But if Todd was involved in running women, then Pete's motive became stronger. Who wouldn't want to keep their daughter away from a pimp?

Shantel called the tow truck and had Todd's car taken to our impound lot. It would be easier to vacuum and process the car there.

When we were done at the house, we taped up Todd's room and a portion of the backyard. We gave David, Dereck and Anna back their phones and strict instructions not to disturb any of the taped-off areas.

Just as we were leaving the house, we got a call from Todd's mother. Sandy had done the next-of-kin notification earlier and his mother was calling now to let us know that she was driving up from Ocala tonight and wanted to meet with us in the morning.

Cara was waiting for me at home. Working at the veterinary clinic and being a kind and gregarious person, she had developed an extensive network of friends in the county. I wasn't surprised that her personal grapevine had been hard at work. When I entered the house, she already had a good idea of what I had been working on and all of the implications that the case could have for Pete.

Cara gave me an affectionate kiss while Alvin, her Pug, sniffed my feet and Ivy, my tabby cat, stared daggers at me from the back of the couch. Ivy was still learning to share my attention.

"I cooked Spanish bean soup so that it wouldn't matter when you got home. And there's fresh brown bread too." The aroma of the soup was comforting. A great, if superficial, reminder of how lucky I was to have Cara in my life.

"I can use some food," I told her.

I was grateful that Cara didn't bombard me with questions as soon as I got home. She let me finish my bowl of soup and a good bit of the bread before bringing up the murder.

"This must be awful for Pete and his family," she said after we'd settled down on the couch.

"It's bad news no matter which way you look at it. Dad and the department are between a rock and a hard place. If he had decided to turn it all over to FDLE, then it would have made him look weak. It would be like admitting that he doesn't think we can properly investigate the case. But with us handling most of it, at some point someone is going to question our impartiality."

"I saw the video. It's pretty bad."

"I know. The longer it takes to find the killer, the harder it's going to be for Pete to get the stench off of him."

"Must be tough for you too."

"I've never had this hard of a time focusing on the victim. I keep worrying about Pete, and how the evidence is going to affect him and his family. I'm worried about what we're going to find on Todd's and Jenny's phones."

"Why?"

"There are probably a number of texts between them. Who knows what we'll find? Unfortunately people, particularly young people, aren't very discreet about what they put in a text message. Of course, there's also Twitter and Facebook and who knows what other social media crap that could be awful for Jenny and Pete if it's made public."

"True."

"I just don't understand how Jenny got mixed up with this character," I said thoughtfully.

"People can be really good at hiding who they really are. How many people get married and find out after they move in together that the other person is too annoying to live with?" Cara asked and I thought I could hear a subtle subtext.

Cara had been bringing more and more stuff over to my place lately. I'd given her a key a couple of months ago and, ever since, I'd felt a bit like I was headed down a steep mountain and I didn't know if my brakes would work.

"What?" Cara asked, having used her superior female radar to detect that my brain had started ruminating on something other than the topic we'd been discussing.

"Nothing," I said in a classic male reply.

"What are you thinking?"

"Nothing in particular," I doubled down. "Just tired." A classic diversion.

We watched part of a Will Ferrell movie before Cara decided to pop open the can of worms that I had been trying hard to keep closed.

"My lease is up at the end of next month," she said and the elephant in the room instantly materialized.

I sat there, not saying a word. My mind went through my complete vocabulary and reviewed all of my past experiences with females, and nowhere did I find a response that could defuse the situation. I stared at the movie and prayed that we wouldn't really have to get into a full-blown discussion tonight.

My silence seemed to be working. I could tell that Cara was trying to decide how far she should push the subject. *Come on, Ferrell, do something to distract her*, I thought.

Alvin came to the rescue, jumping up on the couch between us and snuggling down. The mood shifted and Cara let it go.

I had mixed feelings on top of mixed feelings about the topic. On the one hand, I really enjoyed being around Cara and I seriously believed we might have something that was coming close to a long-term commitment. But, on the other hand, my few experiences with live-in girlfriends weren't good. Two had just turned into soul-crushing experiences that had led to both of us being glad to escape the company of the other, and the last had been a complete disaster. And no matter how much I tried to convince myself that living with Cara would be different, I still couldn't help flinching at the thought.

Though Cara had dropped the subject, my mind was less cooperative. What would it be like when this was no longer a couple-of-times-a-week thing? Would it seem as special having her next to me in bed? Would I grow tired of it? How would I deal with all the little annoyances of having another person in the house? My mind spun with the pros and cons.

CHAPTER FIVE

I was up early and saw Cara and Alvin on their way. Being able to occasionally have Alvin with her at the vet was a perk of her job.

I decided to stop by Dad's on my way into the office. I thought he might want an update on the investigation and, honestly, I just wanted to make sure that he was comfortable with how we were moving forward. I didn't want him having a knee-jerk reaction and taking me off of the case entirely.

Dad had lived alone on his small farm since my mom died. He had recently started dating a woman who'd been my babysitter when I was a kid. She lived in Tallahassee now and managed an upscale restaurant. She was a nice woman, but, of course, she wasn't my mother, and I figured Dad was just looking for a little companionship.

When I pulled into his driveway, I saw a car I didn't recognize parked next to his truck and I wondered who could be visiting him at this time of the morning. Being the sheriff in a rural county, the neighbors had a tendency to just drop by his place whenever they had a problem.

The garage was open so I went to the door that led into the kitchen. I gave a quick knock, heard Mauser's water-buffalo-sized bark from inside and let myself in. What I saw almost caused me to step back outside and look around to make sure I was at the right house.

Sitting at the kitchen table were my dad and Genie Anderson, his girlfriend. While they both had plenty of clothes on, thank God, it was clear from what they were wearing that both of them had woken up in the house that morning. Sitting on the far side of the table, looking like the favored child, was Mauser. The traitor didn't even come over and greet me.

"Morning," Dad said while mopping egg yolk off of his plate with a piece of toast. He was smiling widely, which in and of itself was both unusual and unnerving.

"Yeah," I managed to say.

"You know Genie," he said.

She smiled at me. "Good morning." Was there a little blush to her cheeks?

I was really glad that I hadn't had anything greasy for breakfast. If I had, I don't think I could have held it down.

"I...talk... the case," I stammered, wanting to turn and run, but realizing that that wouldn't have been the adult thing to do.

"Do you want some eggs?" Genie asked me, getting up from the table. She was wearing sweatpants, a sweater and slippers. The slippers were the irrefutable proof that she had slept there. *How often do you have to sleep somewhere before you bring your slippers with you?* I wondered.

"Oh, no. I'm fine." I rummaged around inside my head, trying to find the mature Larry who recognized that his dad was an autonomous adult who could have a relationship with a woman if he chose. Mature Larry was doing a very good job of hiding from me.

Dad could see my discomfort and was doing nothing to help me. He looked me square in the eye and I could see the pleasure that my pain was giving him. After a few moments that seemed more like hours, he finally took pity on me.

"Genie, would you mind? I think Larry wants to talk about the recent murder."

"I am so sorry that your friend is caught up in that. Of course, I'll go up and get dressed." She leaned over and gave Dad a quick and affectionate kiss on the lips that made every fiber of my being cringe.

"Sit down," Dad said and pushed a plate with a couple pieces of toast on it in my direction. "I can't believe that you would let this bother you. You're a big boy." Then he paused and looked at me, his eyes softening for just a moment. "It's been over ten years, Larry."

I swallowed back the lump that had suddenly formed in my throat and took a deep breath. "You're right. It's early and I was just surprised, that's all."

As soon as I was sitting down, Mauser came over and laid his head on my lap as though to apologize to me, when what he really wanted was for me to give him some of the toast.

"Don't think I'm going to forgive you any time soon," I told the big goofball, who kept shifting his eyes toward the toast. "How much have you had already?"

"Only a couple of pieces," Dad said, finishing his eggs and pushing his plate away, all business now. "What have you learned so far?"

"Looks like Todd is going to give us lots of suspects. He had dealings with prostitutes, a grating personality and a quasi-transient lifestyle."

"Dealings?"

"He might have been a driver and security, or possibly more, for at least one woman." The driver/security job was a lot more common now that more sex workers were finding their customers through online sources like craigslist and Tinder. The full-blown purple hat, pink Cadillac pimp was going the way of the dinosaur.

"Evidence?"

"So far no obvious murder weapon and no wallet-dropped-at-the-scene sort of thing." I didn't need to tell him that it would be days and weeks before we sorted through all of the possible evidence and narrowed it down to probable items, which would then have to be sent off to labs where it could be weeks or months before the results came back.

"What are you thinking?" He was deferring to me more than usual. Maybe his having a girlfriend wasn't such a bad thing.

"That all of this is bad news for Pete. Nothing points toward a quick solution."

"You haven't talked to all of Harper's friends yet. Maybe there is an obvious suspect."

"We can hope."

"I did exchange some texts with a friend who's a senior-level advisor with FDLE. He said that they'd be able to prioritize our lab work."

"That can't hurt."

"But they can't spare any manpower. The state budget is too tight. He said that even if we turned the whole case over to them due to conflict of interest, they would only be able to give it the required attention. Nothing extra. They just don't have the resources to deal with a case like this when they're having to investigate serial killers, major drug operations and terrorist threats, plus all the personnel work they have to do for the governor and visiting dignitaries."

"I understand. And, of course, we're shorthanded because Pete's suspended."

"I'll push Major Parks to get through his investigation as quickly as possible. If Pete's cleared, or at least given a minor punishment for the incident at the game, and you and Darlene can provide me with one or two likely suspects, then I could justify reinstating him."

Feeling ignored by us and no doubt unhappy with the downer vibe, Mauser decided to liven up the party by snatching a piece of toast from the plate with his giant maw. After much yelling and shaming, we managed to get back a soggy quarter of the slice of bread. Dad patted him and told him he was a good boy for eventually relinquishing the masticated piece of bread. I just rolled my eyes.

"I've got to get to work." I wanted to get away before Genie came back.

"Good luck. Let me know if you all need anything."

I passed Jamie, Mauser's babysitter, in the yard on my way out to my car. "I think your boy needs some more work," I told him, meaning Dad as much as Mauser.

"What'd the big oaf do this morning?" Jamie asked. I almost smiled thinking of him referring to Dad as a big oaf. I gave him a rundown of Mauser's table manners and he promised to do some more work with the resist command.

On the way to the office, I realized that I probably should have talked to Darlene before talking to Dad, since she was the lead investigator on the case. As a peace offering, I swung by the Donut Hole and got her a couple of fresh apple fritters, her favorite.

She accepted the fritters in the spirit that they were presented and waved off the breach of protocol. "I'm glad you talked to him," she said, picking the apple fritter apart as she ate it. "All last night I tried to think of the best way to get a scent to follow. I think today we need to reach out to Miss Hex and the rest of Todd's friends and family."

"When's the mother going to be here?"

"I got a text from her and they're supposed to be here at nine. We have the autopsy at one and then I figure we can try and find the mysterious Hex."

I agreed. Looking at my watch, I saw that it was already almost nine. "I'll go up front and meet Todd's mother," I told Darlene, who looked grateful.

"Let me know when they're here. We'll talk to them in the small conference room."

Standing at the entrance to the office looking out, I saw Todd's mother approaching with an older woman walking just behind her. From the similarities between the two, it wasn't hard to figure out that they were related and, from the age difference, I assumed that they were mother and daughter. Grief was deeply etched into their features. Something about the way they carried themselves said that this was not the first tragedy they had endured together.

Grief is the hardest emotion to deal with. You want to scream or hit something or change the world or simply give up. But nothing feels right. The world is no longer the world you wanted to live in, but there is no going back. No way to reverse the terrible wrong that you feel has occurred. All you can do is move forward and hope that the pain will hurt less in the future.

I opened the door for the two women.

"Mrs. Harper, I'm Deputy Larry Macklin, one of the investigators looking into your son's murder."

"Bell. Ms. Lorraine Bell. Harper was my ex-husband's name. This is my mother, Rita Bell."

I led them into the small conference room and asked if I could get them anything. When they declined I went out to find Darlene. After introductions were made, Darlene sat down at the table and looked Lorraine in the eye.

"I want you to know that I have no higher priority than finding the person who murdered your son and bringing him to justice." I knew that Darlene was telling the woman the gospel truth. "I also know that finding the murderer will in no way compensate you for your loss."

"Thank you. And I'll be equally honest with you. I want to see that person injected or electrocuted or shot or whatever is done to take their life like they've taken my son's. Todd wasn't perfect. I know that. But he was my son." As she said this, her mother put her hand on her daughter's shoulder. Lorraine shrugged it off. "I don't care what dirty laundry we air or what rocks we have to look under. I want the murderer found and I want him to suffer."

"Good," Darlene said. "Knowing that you are committed to this investigation will help me do my job. We're going to start out with some questions that you might think are wasting time, but the truth is that we have to know your son before we can find out why someone killed him and who that person is."

"I understand. Ask me anything. Take as much time as you want. I have nowhere to go and nothing else to do."

"You're divorced?" Darlene asked, and I saw the muscles under Lorraine's eye twitch.

"Fifteen years." She paused and then went on, "I guess you need to know about him. Clint Harper. A worthless, loveless man. He lives in Seattle. I don't think you need to waste much time on him. He never did care a whit about our son. You know how you tell kids that it's not their fault that their parents are getting a divorce? Our divorce wasn't Todd's fault, but it *was* because I gave birth to him. As soon as I had Todd, Clint lost interest in me. He didn't want any part of family life. I want to blame him for everything, but the truth is, he'd been honest with me. He told me he never wanted kids. All my friends told me he'd change his mind once he saw his son. I thought he couldn't help but love him. How can you hold that tiny baby in your arms and not care about him, not want to protect him and give him a better life? Clint hated everything about children. I don't think he held Todd more than a couple of times."

"He was the coldest man I ever met, and I've met some real icebergs," her mother chimed in. "You stayed with him longer than I would have," Rita said, and Lorraine nodded her head.

"Anyway, he sent the money he was required to and that was all. Never a card, a letter or a phone call to me or Todd from the day he walked out of the house. So I don't think you have to look at him. I haven't even bothered to tell him."

My opinion of Todd was softening a little. What kind of childhood could he have had? Who wouldn't be affected by a father who rejected him completely?

Lorraine went on to talk about the trouble Todd had had with school. "He liked to go to school, but he didn't care about his classes. He just liked the social aspect. He made friends easily, but lost them just as fast. He didn't take anything seriously. Liked the girls. Maybe liked them a little too much."

"Was there ever any trouble?" I asked.

"Twice. The first time was when he was a sophomore in high school. There was an older girl he really liked. Had a crush on her. But she didn't want to have anything to do with him. The more she pushed him away, the more he wanted her to like him. Todd could be lazy as sin, but if he got it into his head that he wanted something, then watch out. Her father caught him watching their house from the bushes one night and called the police. The police talked to Todd, but he wouldn't stop. He was more careful, but he only stopped when she graduated and moved away."

"You said there was another incident."

"Yes," she said hesitantly. "I..."

"Lorraine, that's not important. It has nothing to do with—"

Her mother's words seemed to steel her resolve. "I'm not going to hold anything back. We don't know what's important and what isn't." I was starting to admire Lorraine. "When he was a senior, he went on a couple of dates with a freshman. Apparently he got a little too... fresh. God, that's a stupid, outdated word. He tried to put his hand under her skirt one evening. She didn't want him to, and she slapped him. Thank goodness that did stop him. But, naturally, she didn't want to see him anymore. Her father, who'd never been happy with the relationship, got a restraining order against him when Todd kept going over to her house. I tried to stop him. I even told him that I wasn't going to help him if he landed in jail. But he just wouldn't stop. Pushed too far, the father beat him up. Really... it was horrible."

"What did you do?" Darlene asked.

"The father called me and told me to come get my son. It broke my heart to see him like that, but I wouldn't help Todd press charges. I told him that he had gotten a beating that was deserved and that he should take it like a man."

"I supported the decision," her mother chimed in, looking as hard and chiseled as one of the heads on Mount Rushmore.

"I hated to see him in pain, but his behavior scared me. I

was both angry and grateful that the girl's father did that to him."

"Were there any other times that Todd acted inappropriately toward women?"

"Not that I know of."

"Did he ever try and contact either of the women again?"

"No. I don't think he would do that. It was like he was under a spell when he was obsessed with them. Once the spell was broken, it was broken. He didn't want to even hear their names afterward."

"Why did he move up here?"

"He wanted to go to Florida State, but his grades weren't good enough so he got into Tallahassee Community College with the hopes that he could transfer to FSU after a year or two."

"How was he doing at TCC?"

"Not very good. He never finished anything. He would start the semester talking about how good the classes were, and he'd do okay for a while, but then he'd get bored and drop out. I think he only managed to get a couple of credits," Lorraine said. Behind her, I could see her mother shaking her head.

"Do you know of anyone that might have wanted to hurt him? Someone with a grudge?"

"I really don't think that the girls or their families could have had anything to do with this. All of that was years ago."

"Anyone else?"

"I just don't know. I... well, I know he did drugs. I confronted him once when I found some pot in his room. Not much, just a small baggie. We had a talk and he admitted that he did some other drugs sometimes. Ecstasy, stuff like that, but he swore he didn't have a problem with it. I worked at a rehab center for almost a decade. I know what an addict looks like. I believed him."

Todd's father might have been an ass, but his mother seemed like one of the most centered people I'd ever met. I'd say Todd had scored one out of two in the parent department.

"Can you think of anyone he talked about? Good or bad," Darlene asked.

His mother mentioned Dereck and Jenny, as well as a couple of other names that I wrote down. We had asked Shantel to make his phone a high priority, and she'd assured me that we'd be able to get the information off of it this morning.

"I saw that video," Lorraine said in a neutral tone. "I understand that man is a deputy with your department?"

"He is. Pete Henley's his name. He's on paid leave until the matter at the school is thoroughly investigated and we can be reasonably sure that he had nothing to do with your son's murder." I desperately wanted to plead Pete's case to these women, but I knew the argument would come off as nothing more than the thin blue line defending one of its own.

"I want you to know that I'm no fool. I'm going to be watching the investigation. I want my son's killer found, no matter who it is."

"The sheriff has asked the Florida Department of Law Enforcement to help in the investigation in order to ensure that we're not overlooking anything or favoring one of our own," Darlene assured her.

"Ha, the state. I'm not impressed with the state's ability to oversee anything."

"We're going to hire our own investigator," Rita said.

I cringed, not seeing how that would help anything. "I would suggest that you wait a little while. Right now we are just getting to some of the witnesses, and having a third party interfering could cause problems."

"I'm not threatening to hire someone. I'm telling you that we're going to do it," Lorraine's mother said firmly.

"And I'm not threatening you when I tell you that if a third party interferes in any way with this investigation, they will be arrested and charged with obstruction," Darlene said with a firmness that was equal to the old woman's. Softening a bit, she said, "Give us a little time. And if you think it's necessary to take on a private investigator, I'll be glad to talk to them and make sure he or she knows where the lines are drawn. I'll also personally provide any information that I can." Darlene took out her cards and handed one to each of the women. "That's my direct cell phone number. I'll be glad to talk to you at any time."

We went over a few more details before escorting the women out to their car. Watching them drive away, I was glad that Darlene was the lead on the case. I thought it would be much easier for them to trust her than me.

CHAPTER SIX

It was eleven o'clock when we got a call from Marcus telling us that our IT guy had transferred everything on Todd's SIM card to a file and that he was sending it over to us. Darlene and I split up the responsibility for going through the data. I took text messages from the last month while she went through all the contacts, recent calls and messages.

I found exactly what I was afraid of in the text messages. Lots of messages back and forth between Jenny and Todd, and few of them were good news. Recent ones were mostly Todd begging to see her and Jenny telling him no. Mixed in were several where Jenny had told Todd that her father was a deputy and was mad that Todd kept pestering her. One explicitly said that Pete had threatened to teach Todd a lesson if he came around to Jenny's house again.

The texts between Hex and Todd talked about times and places to meet up. It didn't take an expert to read between the lines. Todd drove Hex to meetings with clients, then hung around to make sure she was okay. He got paid by the hour, plus gas money. All very professional. He'd also done some similar jobs for a friend of Hex's called Sunny. But Todd complained that Sunny was too bossy and wasted his time. The arrangement with her had ended long before the murder.

I also found a number of messages from Dereck and David, mostly following the general theme of: *Where the hell is the money for…?* Other than that, there were the usual texts from a few friends looking to meet for a beer, go to a club or play a video game mixed with a few cryptic messages that probably referred to the purchase of drugs.

When we were both done, Darlene and I compared notes.

"Nothing good for Pete," she said. "There isn't anything in the texts or contacts to suggest anyone else had a motive." I had to agree with her.

We decided to pick up lunch in Tallahassee on the way to the autopsy. I called Hex, the text messages having revealed that she lived there. She'd already heard about Todd's murder and agreed to meet us around three.

"She actually sounded glad I'd called. Prostitutes must be getting friendlier," I said.

"Sex worker. I went to a seminar a year ago that talked about cyber crimes. A lot of young people are paying their bills by doing sex work on the side. These women aren't cut from the same cloth as the crack whores who are enslaved to a pimp. These are just regular people trying to get by. Most of the time, if they have dealings with the cops it's as victims, not criminals."

"Damn dangerous work. Of course, that's why she was using Todd."

"Exactly. She's probably scared as hell that it has something to do with her business."

We rode in silence for a little bit.

"You know, you haven't insulted me in more than twelve hours."

"I know, Rookie. I don't kick someone when they're down. I'll be honest with you. I can't really wrap my head around Pete being the killer either. I'm not saying it isn't possible. I think he'd be pretty brutal to someone who hurt his kids, but that didn't happen. The motive looks good on paper, or I should say on video, but in reality... I don't know."

"Thanks for that. Hey, you know, maybe we should follow up on the videos. There were several people taking pictures and videoing the argument. Maybe one of them posted it for a reason."

"You think someone might have wanted to show that Pete had a motive for killing Todd?" Darlene asked.

"Perhaps. Just a possibility." I shrugged.

"Sure, why not?"

Darlene and I grabbed lunch at Cabos Island Bar and Grill. While we waited for our food, I called our IT guy and asked him to trace the origin of as many of the video and photo postings on social media as he could find.

"You know, I trust Dr. Darzi. I really don't know why we need to look over his shoulder," I complained as we ate. I really wasn't in the mood to watch him take Todd's body apart.

"Don't be so squeamish. Keep your eyes open and you might learn something."

"Back to insulting me. I feel better already," I kidded her.

Down in Dr. Darzi's white sterile dungeon, we found him supervising a pair of interns as they wheeled in the body, still in the body bag, and transferred it to the stainless steel table.

"Remember, the pathologist only gets credit when he screws up," Darzi told the two young men, who looked as if they expected to screw up and were just waiting for it to happen.

"You," he said, pointing to the dark-haired one, "can stay and assist." He turned to us. "Come in. I'll be ready in a minute."

Ten minutes later, he was picking over Todd's body while it was still clothed. "The pants are unzipped," Darzi pointed out. With gloved hands, he carefully searched all of the pockets, turning them inside out and collecting any lint and debris he uncovered. There was a five-dollar bill in one of the pockets, but no wallet, keys or phone. We'd found all three in his room.

"He wasn't planning on going anywhere when he stepped out back," I said.

"Probably peeing outdoors, just like David," Darlene said in a boys-will-be-boys tone.

Darzi and his intern carefully removed Todd's clothes. Once the body was lying nude on the table, Darzi stepped back and scanned the corpse, then he focused on the large dented-in area of the scalp.

"The victim was hit from behind on the right side. I'd say that the first strike would probably have been fatal by itself. But once the victim was on the ground, he was struck by a couple more blows that thoroughly crushed in the right side of the forehead."

"Any idea of the size and shape of the object used?"

"Large and rounded. At least two or three inches across. I'll be able to give you more exact measurements later. There are no defensive wounds," he observed as he looked the body over again, lifting the hands and turning them. "I think I would be justified in saying that he never saw the blow coming."

"Someone came up from behind him and hit him with an... object." I was sure that Darlene had almost said "bat," which is what we all were envisioning. "No warning. Probably no conversation."

"Very cold-blooded," I said, trying to imply that Pete would not be capable of something like that.

"I understand that Deputy Henley could be involved," Darzi said matter-of-factly. "He's a tall man. I should be able to tell you how he would have held the object and swung it. Of course, I could be much more precise if I could examine the weapon."

I saw where he was going. Hopefully we'd never get to the point where Pete was on trial, but if it appeared that he would have had to swing the murder weapon from an awkward and unnatural position; that could help his case.

Smaller details have gotten people off.

We left the hospital not knowing much more than when we had arrived.

"I hate to say it, but I really think we're looking for a baseball bat," Darlene said.

"I hate it even more that I have to agree with you. If we assume that Pete didn't kill Todd, then someone might have been purposefully trying to frame him."

"Which means that it probably wasn't a drug deal gone bad or something that grew out of the two stalking incidents when he was younger."

"Yeah, drug dealers wouldn't care. And what are the odds that someone who's held a grudge for years would see the video and think that Saturday night was the perfect time to put an end to Todd's existence?"

We were right on time to meet with Hex. She was living in a dodgy apartment complex on the west side of Tallahassee near the community college campus. She'd told me that her real name was Jane Lindsey. She opened the door on the first knock.

"Come in," she said, looking embarrassed and worried at the same time. She was very petite. Only five feet tall and not much more than a hundred pounds. Her black hair was pulled back in a ponytail.

She offered us a seat in the living room, which was very neat and clean. "I can't believe that Todd is… that someone killed him."

"How long had you known Todd?" Darlene asked.

"I met him at school last year. We were both in Psychology 101. We went out a couple times, but we didn't really click romantically. But we did become good friends."

"How long had you all worked together?" I asked.

This caused her to pause. I could see her trying to decide how much we knew about what she did, and how much she wanted us to know.

"I'll save you some trouble. We know that you have been doing sex work and that Todd was helping you out."

She looked like she was going to protest and I held up my hand to stop her.

Darlene stepped in with, "We don't care about any of that except for how it relates to Todd's murder."

Jane was young and naive, so it didn't take her long to believe us. "He's been driving me for about six months. It works out well for both of us. He is… wasn't very interested in a nine-to-five job, and I needed a guy who wasn't interested in dating me to drive me to appointments."

"You two got along?"

"He was great. Todd pulled me out of a couple of bad situations. I used another guy before Todd and he would get high while I was… conducting business. If I'd needed him, he wouldn't have been able to do much more than fall down on the ground. Once I even had to drive, he was so wasted. But not Todd. He was really attentive."

"What kind of bad situations?"

"One of them was my fault. I was still pretty new and I hadn't been really clear about the money part. My date thought he shouldn't have to pay full price."

"What did Todd do?"

"At first he came on strong, which was good 'cause the guy was out of control. After the guy calmed down, Todd just spelled it out for him, even pulled up the messages that set the deal up and showed them to the jerk. Guy paid, and we all went our separate ways."

"How long ago was this?"

"Like I said, that was when I was pretty new. Maybe the third time that Todd drove me. Six months ago, maybe?"

"What other confrontations were there?"

"About two months ago, I knocked on a guy's door and he just reached out and pulled me into the house. Like he was grabbing me off of the street or something. Shook me up and, before I could recover, the bastard slammed me down on the ground. He knelt on my back so I couldn't move while he tied me up. I really thought I was going to be raped, maybe killed. But Todd and I had a signal."

61

"A signal?"

"Yeah. When I'd go inside, I'd get specific with the client so we all knew what the deal was. I had learned from that earlier incident not to assume that we'd worked everything out in advance. Anyway, once everything was clear and I felt comfortable, the last thing I'd do before… taking care of the client was to text Todd an all-clear."

"So when he didn't get your text he knew something was wrong?"

"He was like a damn superhero. The guy was on top of me, pressing me down into the carpet, when suddenly, *bam*, the creep was gone. By the time I figured out what was going on, Todd had hit the guy a couple of times with a chair." She was smiling at the memory.

"What happened then?" Darlene asked. She was no doubt thinking the same thing that I was—Todd had hit a man over the head and then was killed by getting hit in the head. Possible connection?

"Todd tied the… Oh, hey, I don't know if I should say anymore." Jane's eyes had widened as she realized that she was talking to a couple of law enforcement officers about taking part in an assault, possibly during the commission of a felony. The felony would depend on proving that she had been there to sell herself for money. If they had tied the man up, then kidnapping could have been added to the charges.

"I understand that you're worried about your liability. You should be. But my partner and I are razor-focused on Todd's murder," I told her.

Darlene looked at me with a thoughtful expression, then added, "Which one of us would you rather talk to? One of us can leave, and then you can tell the other what happened. That way, it will just be your word against whichever one of us hears it. We just need to be able to look into any problems that Todd might have had with other people. We need to figure out who is a suspect in his murder, that's all."

"Like she said. If it turns out that it *does* have something to do with the murder, then you'll be able to decide in the future whether you want to talk about it under oath."

"Yeah, I kinda see that," Jane said. She thought for a moment and then pointed at me. "Okay, I'll talk to him."

Darlene, with good grace, got up and left the apartment.

"You aren't recording this, are you? 'Cause I don't give you permission to record this conversation," Jane said as if she assumed she was already being recorded.

"No recording," I assured her. "Just start where you left off."

"Like I said, it took me a minute to catch my breath. By the time I did, Todd had the guy all tied up."

"Did you call the police?" I asked, already knowing the answer.

"No." She shook her head. "I know, I felt really wrong about it. Took me a long time to get the thought of another woman walking into that same situation out of my head. But I couldn't."

"What else did you all do?"

"Todd did all kinds of crap to him. He took his wallet. Pissed on him. I know, that's gross, but I sure loved watching it. Todd found some paint and wrote 'sick bastard' and some other stuff on his door and outside his house. Finally, when we left, Todd warned him that we had all of his personal information and would screw him over big time if we ever heard of another woman getting messed with." She sighed. "I know we couldn't really follow through on that threat, but it made me feel better."

"We'd like his name, address and any other information you have on him. When was this?"

"Like I said, about two months ago, I guess. Oh, shit, I can tell you exactly." Jane whipped out her phone and started scrolling through it, then held it out to me. "This was the final thing we did to him. We told him we'd post it all over the Internet if he bothered me or anyone else again."

I took the phone and held it so I that could see the image. It was a picture of a man with a wet face and hair. He was in his mid-thirties with some kind of tattoo visible under his shirt collar. He looked very pissed—literally. I noted the time and date on the image and then used my phone to take a photo of the photo.

While I was looking at the phone, Jane had gone and retrieved his wallet. She handed the beat-up leather to me like it was a viper.

"There was fifty-nine dollars in it when we took it. I told Todd that he could have the money, but I replaced it."

Inside was a driver's license for a Samuel Ellison, a gas credit card, an insurance card and a couple of business cards that had variations of Ellison's name with companies that ranged from roofing to plumbing. This did not appear to be the wallet of an upstanding citizen. Maybe, just maybe, we were onto something.

"I'm going to keep this," I told her. "Don't worry, I'm not going to get you into trouble. If anyone asks, I'll say that I found it. I'm going to give you a warning, though. Don't delete that picture. It may be evidence in a murder investigation. Obstructing justice can be a very serious crime." I gave her my sternest look. "We'll keep you out of it if at all possible. Is there anything else before I go get Deputy Marks?"

Jane shook her head meekly.

I felt a little sorry for her and added, "Look on all of this as a bit of penance for not having come forward originally."

She nodded and I brought Darlene back in.

"Can you give us the names of any of Todd's other friends?"

"Gosh, not really. He kind of went through friends. When we first started hanging out we had several mutual friends, but they all got tired of him pretty quickly. Mostly 'cause he was always mooching off of everyone and bragging about it." She got a thoughtful expression on her face. "I think they would have put up with one or the other, but the combination got old real fast."

We took down a few of the names anyway, thanked her for her help and left.

Before we drove out of the parking lot, I plugged Mr. Ellison's stats into my laptop and got back a nice set of priors which included burglary, fraud, battery, drunk and disorderly, trespassing, and the fact that he was currently serving probation for check fraud. His address was in a Section 8 housing complex on the south side of Tallahassee.

"May as well swing by and see if our new person of interest is home," Darlene said.

As soon as we pulled past the apartment complex's office, we started getting "the look" from people sitting on their porches or standing in the parking lot. *Who are they after now?* the faces seemed to be asking.

It's a fallacy that most of the people in public housing are criminals. The vast majority are simply low-income folks who have no other option. In Tallahassee, about a third of the residents are older people who have worked hard all of their lives, but are stuck trying to survive on the subsistence money that Social Security sends to them. Another third are people who will only be there for six months or a year until they get back on their feet—women or single mothers who need to save a little money before they can move out, or a family where one or both of the parents are between jobs. It's the last group, people who have drug, psychiatric or behavioral issues, that provide the stereotype for public housing. But, regardless of how law-abiding they are, almost all of the residents have had confrontations with law enforcement at some time or another. So we got the look.

It was almost five o'clock when we pulled up to apartment 421. A mix of cars was parked out in front of the building, but knocking didn't produce an answer. I put my ear to the door.

"Nothing."

"I'll contact his parole officer in the morning. If we don't hear back soon, we can push the issue."

I thought about knocking on the neighbors' doors, but there wasn't any sense in spreading the word that we were looking for Ellison.

I dropped Darlene off at the office and headed home. I knew that Cara was going to be there, so I made a pit-stop for a six-pack of microbrews. I was hoping that we could just relax. I needed to give my brain a mini-vacation.

We met at my gate. I opened it and Cara stopped for a quick kiss before driving up to my house. I lived in a doublewide on twenty acres that I'd bought shortly after I started working for the department. Whenever I drove from my gate through the canopy of oak trees, I always tried to leave my work behind me. It wasn't always easy.

Cara was waiting for me on the small deck. The last light from the setting sun shown behind her red hair and she literally glowed. *Why wouldn't I want to come home to this every day?* I thought.

Once inside, I told her that I'd fix dinner. "Theirs too," I said, trying to stare down Alvin and Ivy.

"Perfect. I'll go change out of my scrubs."

By the time she'd showered and changed, I'd fried up some catfish that Marcus had given me and made coleslaw and Texas toast to go along with it.

"Damn, you're good," Cara complimented me. "I'll finish up here if you want to go change."

We enjoyed the meal in companionable silence, both of us fending off the occasional paw-swipe from Ivy as she tried to steal pieces of fish off our plates.

"I'm sorry for bringing up the lease thing yesterday," Cara said as she brought the dishes over to the sink where I was washing them. I didn't point out that she was bringing it up again.

"No problem," I said, trying to sound neutral.

"I don't want to rush things," she said, unintentionally leaving me feeling a bit irritated that we were talking about it again.

"It's just the timing," I said, wiping down the cast-iron skillet.

"How's the case coming along?" Cara asked, and I was relieved to be talking about work rather than the moving-in thing.

"We've at least identified another person of interest. Hopefully this lead will take us somewhere."

"Somewhere away from Pete."

"Exactly."

"How's he doing?"

"I don't know. I really shouldn't talk with him. Can I borrow your phone?"

"Sure. But I thought you just said you shouldn't talk to him," she said with raised eyebrows.

"I said 'shouldn't.' Doesn't mean I won't." I put the last dish in the rack to dry and grabbed her phone.

"Hello?" I heard Pete say, not recognizing Cara's number.

"It's me. How's it going?"

"We shouldn't be talking."

"I know, and if they find out I used Cara's phone, it will look all that much more suspicious. The hell with 'em," I said rather cavalierly.

"I'm grilling out. I thought it might cheer everyone up. Not." He sounded pretty depressed, and who could blame him?

"How's Jenny doing?"

"Still mad at me. Frightened. Embarrassed. And probably a couple of other negative feelings and emotions."

"Sarah holding up?"

"Like the trooper she is. But I can tell she's worried. I know how the justice system works, so it's not like I can guarantee to her that everything will be okay."

"We're working on it, buddy," I said, sounding more cheerful than I felt.

"I know. I trust you all. That's not what I meant."

I knew exactly what he meant. There were plenty of innocent men rotting in prison or living on the outside with a dark cloud hanging over their heads because fate had screwed them over.

"And Kim?" I asked, wondering how his youngest was

doing.

"Ha! She's trying to talk me into investigating the murder on my own. With her as my Dr. Watson, of course. I think she actually finds it exciting that we have a murder this close to home. I'm just hoping the reality of the situation doesn't catch up to her." He paused and then added, "I'm really grateful to your father for keeping most of this in-house."

"I know. Hey, we better stop before I start talking about the investigation."

"I hear you. I really appreciate you calling." But he didn't sound like I'd cheered him up much.

"Take care," I told him.

"That didn't sound good," Cara said.

"He's really worried. We've all seen investigations that drag on for years. Hell, there are some that go on for decades."

"There's a lot riding on you and Darlene. I wish there was something I could do for Pete. He's a great teacher. Once I got used to the gun, I've really enjoyed my shooting lessons."

"You know, it might help if you asked him to take you out to the range again. Nothing makes him feel better than getting out and shooting. It would take his mind off of things for a little while, at least."

"I'll give him a call. I've got Thursday off."

"Thank you," I said, leaning over and giving her a kiss. I loved her big heart and generous nature. "Look, give me a couple of days to get a handle on this investigation and then we'll have a talk about the lease situation."

This time she leaned in and kissed me. As it became more passionate, she jumped up and wrapped her legs around my waist and I carried her to bed.

CHAPTER SEVEN

Cara and Alvin were already gone by the time I sat down with my bowl of cereal. Ivy kept me company by trying to stick her nose into my bowl, so I took a spoon and gave her a little of the milk.

"You know, if you'd get into more fights with Alvin, I wouldn't have to make a decision about letting Cara move in." Ivy continued lapping at the milk, ignoring my prattle.

My phone rang, causing me to jump and splash milk on Ivy's nose. "Sorry!" I told her, looking at the phone and not recognizing the number.

"Hello?" I said cautiously.

"Get over here. I don't know what the hell to do!" Pete said. From the trembling fear and confusion in his voice, my mind conjured up images of dead bodies in his backyard.

"What the hell's happened?" I asked, getting up, grabbing my coat and keys and heading for the door. "Is somebody hurt?"

"No. Nobody's hurt. Just get here quick." He sounded dazed.

"On my way." I hung up and realized that he must have used someone else's phone. Probably one of his daughters.

I drove faster than was safe in the early morning fog. I

tried to figure out what could be wrong, and hoped that the truth was less frightful than my imagination. I pulled into Pete's driveway and was out of the car almost before it had stopped moving. I didn't make it two steps before Pete came trotting around the side of the house.

"This way," he said in a loud stage whisper. I gawked at him. He was in boxers and a T-shirt. "Come on back here. Wait, grab a set of gloves first." I went back and pulled some gloves out of the trunk. I noticed that Sarah's car was gone. She worked in Tallahassee and must have already left.

Pete was herding me toward the backyard. The morning was cool and he was underdressed, but I could still see sweat dripping off of his brow. Pete was never nervous. He was our department's designated sniper both for his shooting skills and his calm under pressure. But today he was coming close to a full panic attack.

"Here, here!" he said, pointing toward the large DIY brick grill he'd built two years earlier. Suddenly, he grabbed me. "Don't touch it!"

Had he gone mad? Gotten into some type of drug? He wasn't drunk, I could tell that. I watched as he peered into the ashes that filled the bottom of the grill as though a pit viper might suddenly spring out.

"There. See it?"

There was something in the ashes. "What is it?"

"Look closer."

I leaned in. The sun was still low in the sky and the glare made it difficult to see into the dark recesses of the grill. I bent forward and then I saw it. I jerked upright.

"How the hell did it get in there?" I asked Pete.

"I don't know. I grilled out last night. Just some hamburgers and vegetables, that's all. After Sarah and the kids left this morning, I thought I'd clean out the ashes. That's when I found it. I haven't touched anything."

I put on my rubber gloves and carefully reached in and moved the object just enough to be sure that I'd seen what I thought I'd seen. There was no doubt. It was the knob end of a wooden baseball bat.

"What the hell, Pete?"

"I don't know. Somebody came into my yard last night and put that in my grill. That's the only explanation for it being here," he said, sounding almost hysterical. I couldn't blame him. I was just beginning to see all of the implications.

"Why? Is it the murder weapon? It could just be a prank." I didn't really believe what I was saying.

"I don't think this is a joke," Pete said, speaking out loud what I was thinking. "But if it's the murder weapon, and the killer wants to frame me, why not just put it in my shed and call in an anonymous tip?"

"I don't know."

"If I'd been smart, I would have just poured some lighter fluid over it and burned it the rest of the way up."

"Instead you called me," I said, realizing for the first time what a difficult situation he'd put me in.

"Oh, shit. I wasn't thinking. I guess you need to call in the crime scene techs."

"And arrest you. You know that's what I have to do." I thought about that for a few moments. "That's what I *should* do."

"I haven't given you any choice," he said quietly. "How can everything go so wrong?" Pete looked completely poleaxed. On one hand, I really wished he'd just destroyed the evidence, but on the other hand I realized just how wrong that thought was.

"We need some time to think. If I arrest you now, you'll never get the stink off of you. The media loves the lawman-gone-bad angle. You'll be the headliner in all the Florida papers."

"You aren't making me feel better."

"Think. If that's evidence, we need to have it examined properly."

"Maybe you could wait," he suggested cautiously.

"What do you mean?"

"I don't know. I can't put you in the position of

committing a felony for me."

"Let me decide what I'm willing to do for you. Okay?" I said sternly. "You mean that I could bag it and tag it, but just not log it in?"

"I guess. Look, I don't—"

"Stop it! If you didn't want to get me involved in this mess, then you shouldn't have called me," I said rather harshly. "But you did. So now I get to decide what I want to do."

"I'm sorry." Pete stared down at the ground.

"Hey, what are friends for except to get each other into potentially ten-to-twenty-year situations?" I tried to joke, but it just came out flat. "Preserving the piece of bat is one thing, but the whole area needs to be processed. He, whoever he is, might have left footprints or fingerprints. DNA. What about all of that?" I asked, and all he could do was shrug.

That's when my phone rang. I took it out and looked at it. It was Lt. Johnson, our supervisor. For a moment I had the terrifying feeling that he knew where we were and what we were doing. I took a deep breath and answered it.

"Larry, I hate to do this to you, but I don't have much choice." Again, the thought that Pete and I had been under surveillance and were now both going to be arrested crossed my mind. "We have another murder. I'm making you the lead on it for the time being."

"But Darlene and I need to devote ourselves full time to the Harper murder."

"You think I don't know how important that is?" His voice was rising and taking on the drill sergeant tones that he'd cultivated during his twenty years in the military.

"No, sir. I mean, I know you do."

"With Pete out, we're short-handed. I've already discussed this with the sheriff," he said, letting me know that I couldn't go over his head on this one. "I'm in charge of all aspects of this case. You are not to talk to your father or to Darlene about this murder investigation. Do you understand?"

"No. What do you mean I'm not supposed to talk to Dad or Darlene?" I was being a little dense, but I had never before been told not to discuss a case with my father.

"He is recusing himself from this investigation. Trust me, you'll understand soon enough." He gave me the address and a few of the particulars, then hung up.

I turned back to Pete. "I'll go get a bag for this," I said, nodding toward the piece of baseball bat sitting in the ashes.

Pete started to say something, but I stopped him. "I don't have time to argue or think of something better. After I'm gone, go ahead and see what you can find in the way of evidence. It won't be admissible and we won't even be able to tell anyone where we got it. But at least we'll have it."

The location of the latest murder was in one of the best neighborhoods in Calhoun, with large, stately homes that dated back to the nineteenth century. Located close to downtown and the courthouse square, a lot of the county's lawyers and city officials lived in the neighborhood.

As soon as I turned onto Washington Street, I saw the patrol cars and an ambulance parked in front of a large Victorian house with a wrap-around porch. I got a chill when I realized who lived in the two-story white Colonial next door. Charles Maxwell, Calhoun's chief of police, had lived there with his wife ever since they'd moved to Adams County. And next door, the house with the patrol cars, was the home of a county judge—or, I should say, the home of a late judge. His wife, Madge Baxter, still lived there. The judge had been a kindly man, but his wife was a notorious battle-axe.

I realized that Maxwell must have somehow been involved. He was running against Dad for sheriff in the upcoming fall election, which would explain why Dad couldn't be active in the investigation. And Darlene had worked for Maxwell as a police officer before she joined our department. Having left on friendly terms, she could've been seen as being biased.

I parked and saw Deputy Derick Jacobs, who had been first on the scene from our department. He came trotting over to me as I got out of my car.

"I've set up a perimeter with our guys. I've had to wave off some of the city police. Naturally, they all want to know what's going on with their boss."

"Facts first. Who's the victim?"

"Old Mrs. Baxter. She was found this morning by her maid."

"Where's the body?" I asked, walking toward the house.

"Outside by the back door. Pruning shears in her back."

"You're kidding?" The whole thing was beginning to sound like a game of Clue.

"'Fraid not. Shantel and Marcus are on their way. It looks like she was killed first thing this morning. You can see her footprints in the dew and someone else's." He saw my look. "Don't worry, I took a ton of pictures of the footprints. Even put my baton in a couple of the pictures for perspective."

"Good job."

We'd come to the edge of the crime scene tape. As much as I wanted to go look at the scene, I knew I had to wait for Shantel and Marcus to document it.

"Where's the maid?"

"She's with the paramedics. Almost hysterical. Her name's Mrs. Carrillo."

As we neared the ambulance, I could see a middle-aged Hispanic woman sitting on a stretcher. Her face was buried in a towel, but I could hear her moaning from twenty yards away.

I nodded to the EMTs and knelt down beside Mrs. Carrillo.

"I know this is hard, but I need to ask you a few questions."

She mumbled something that sounded, to my untrained ears, like a prayer in Spanish before she opened her eyes and looked at me.

"I cannot believe it." Her eyes were wide and red from crying. "Mrs. Baxter. Who would do this?"

That's the million-dollar question, I thought. "Tell me everything you did from the time you arrived at the house. Start with how you got here. What time was it?"

"My son, he drop me off every morning. At nine o'clock. I want to come earlier, but Mrs. Baxter, she likes her morning time. Told me nine and no earlier. So if I'm early, I wait until nine. This morning, I was right on time. I went up to the house and the door, it was unlocked. Mrs. Baxter say, if the door is locked, just go home. I get paid for the day. The door has only been locked a couple of times when she's been sick and didn't want to be bothered. And she pay me, just like she says."

"But the door was unlocked this morning."

"That's right. I go in like I always do. I hang my sweater up. Next I listen for Mrs. Baxter. But I no hear anything, so I just get to work in the kitchen."

"What did you do in the kitchen?"

"I sweep and then put any dirty dishes in the sink. Once I do that, I turn the water on until it is good and hot."

"Did you notice anything unusual? Maybe an extra glass or plate? Food lying out?" I hoped that she hadn't washed evidence.

"No. Mrs. Baxter's coffee cup and plate were on the table like most mornings. When I went to the sink, I look out in the backyard. I like that. Every morning I wash the dishes and look out on the beautiful yard. But I seen something. Something I knew was wrong."

"What did you see?"

Her eyes were big as she remembered. "I thought that it was a sheet or a tablecloth that had blown off a line or something. But it shouldn't have been there. I turned the water off and went out the back door. That's when…" Mrs. Carrillo began rocking back and forth, moaning. "…poor Mrs. Baxter. Horrible. Horrible."

"Please, if you could, just tell me what you saw."

"On the ground. Lying there in her robe with those things, big things, sticking out of her back."

"What did you do then?"

She crossed herself. "I screamed. I screamed and ran back into the house. I tried to use my phone, but my hands were shaking so bad I couldn't make it work. I run outside and over to Mr. Maxwell's house. I know he is big man in the police department. Mrs. Baxter is always talking about him."

"What happened when you went to his house?"

"He was there and I told him what happened. He went to look for himself and then he came back and said that the police and doctors were on the way."

I had noticed Shantel and Marcus show up while I was talking to Mrs. Carrillo. I excused myself, leaving her in the hands of the medics.

Shantel looked tired. "Has the world gone mad?" she asked me.

"Yes," was my simple answer. "You can start photographing and videotaping. Coroner is on his way."

"The way you're going, you'll soon be able to have your own film library. Macklin Murder Scene Films," Marcus said.

"Excuse me while I don't laugh."

They unloaded their equipment and got started while I contemplated my next move. I needed to go talk to Maxwell, but I didn't want to. The man was an ass. With no choice, I sighed and headed up his driveway.

As soon as I stepped up on the brick porch, the front door opened and there he stood in his uniform, decorated with enough gold and ribbons for the New York City police chief.

"Macklin? You're the best they could send?"

"I'm going to assume that's a rhetorical question."

"Seriously, are you the lead investigator or do they just have you doing some of the interviews?"

"I'm getting neck strain looking up at you," I said, ignoring him. At 6'6", Maxwell was one of the few people that towered over my six feet even. However, the only way I had ever looked up to him was physically. "Can we go inside and talk?"

He looked like someone who had to decide whether or not to let a rain-soaked stray dog into the house. "I suppose," he finally allowed.

Maxwell had a good ol' boy routine that he frequently turned on for the locals in Calhoun, but he was originally from Orlando, his family was wealthy and he'd studied pre-law at Emory before deciding on a law enforcement career. He always dropped the pretense with Dad and me and never hesitated to let us know how little he thought of us.

The house was immaculate and beautifully decorated. He led me into the dining room to a table that could seat twelve easily. He waved toward a chair and we both sat down.

"Could you give me an outline of the events of this morning?"

"Yes," he said and smiled.

Asshole, I thought. "Then do it," I said and let a beat pass before I added, "Please."

"My wife got up at seven and fixed breakfast. I got up at eight and came down to eat. At nine my wife left for work, and I went back upstairs to get dressed to go to the station. So far, nothing unusual. But before I could finish dressing, I heard a woman scream. I couldn't understand what she was saying, but it sounded like it was coming from the front of the house and getting closer. I went to our bedroom window and looked out to see a plump, middle-aged woman trotting up our drive waving her hands. I grabbed my robe and went down to see what the problem was. She was pounding on the door by the time I got down the stairs."

"Had you ever met the woman before today?" I asked, and he actually seemed to take a moment to think about it.

"I think I've seen her coming and going from Madge Baxter's house. I don't know her name or anything else about her."

"So you opened the door…"

"And she was yelling incoherently. I kept telling her to calm down. It took me a minute or two to get her to talk slowly enough for me to figure out that Madge was lying on the ground in her backyard. At that point, I had the woman sit down on the bench on my porch while I went to see about Madge."

"Had Mrs. Carrillo told you anything about the condition of the body?"

"Probably, but I couldn't understand half of what she was saying. She was speaking in a mix of English and Spanish, and very fast. All I knew when I went over to check on Madge was that she was lying on the ground in the backyard."

"You went over to her house?"

"Since I knew she was in the backyard, I cut through the alley that runs behind our houses and came into her backyard that way. I didn't have to get too close to the body to see what the situation was. The large pair of pruning shears sticking out of her back was a big clue. Once I'd made an assessment of the situation, I came back here and called dispatch."

"You didn't approach the body to see if she was still alive?"

He sighed. "I considered it. But looking at the body from twelve feet away, it was clear that she had stopped bleeding, indicating that her heart had stopped beating. From the look of her glazed eyes, it was pretty clear she'd been dead for a while."

"You came straight back here? You didn't touch anything else in her yard?"

"The only thing I touched was the gate that leads from her yard to the alley."

"Who arrived on scene first?"

"One of my officers, Cecil Ryan. But by the time he'd arrived, I'd already realized that my officers shouldn't be involved."

"Why?" I asked.

He responded with a deep sigh. "I'm surprised you don't know. Your father is probably aware of it." He stopped and seemed to be gathering his thoughts, or possibly his emotions. "I've been engaged in a very public fight with Madge. The alley behind our houses was used for decades as a way for workers to pick up our garbage and for salesmen to deliver meat, bread, milk and produce. Now, no one but miscreants uses the alley. We have to take our garbage cans to the curb, just like everyone else in town. No one delivers food to our kitchens anymore. The alley is an eyesore and just provides an opportunity for thieves and vandals.

"So I've gotten all the people who live on this block to agree to close the alley and divide the property between us. Everyone except Mrs. Baxter, who seemed to think that the good old days when you could tell servants and tradesmen to use the back entrance were going to make a comeback."

"And you all argued over this?"

"Yes. At one point we got into a shouting match at a city commission meeting." He seemed uncomfortable admitting all of this. He shifted in his chair and his eyes were looking everywhere but at me. "That's why I thought that your department should handle it. I didn't know they were going to put a junior G-man in charge." Throwing an insult my way seemed to make him feel better.

"Do you know anyone else who would have a motive for killing her?"

"She was a very cantankerous old woman. Some of the other homeowners wanted the alley done away with too. Russell Simmons felt very strongly about it. His house was broken into last year, and they used the alley to do it. I also know that Madge had fights with workmen over money."

"Does she have any family?"

"A sister that lives up in Savannah. Her sister might have children. I don't know. But Madge's husband died several years ago, and their only daughter died of cancer when she was young."

"Do you know if she had much money?"

79

"Not really. She always acted like she was going broke, but you know that her husband was a judge, and her father owned a chain of grocery stores. Word was that they'd left her well set up."

"Of course your fingerprints and DNA are on record." I couldn't resist tossing this on the table. My words had the desired effect. His face turned red.

"You… Yes, I'll provide whatever else you need," he said and stood up. "I'll show you out." The way he said it made it sound more like, *I'll throw you out.*

CHAPTER EIGHT

Leaving Maxwell behind, I went over to check on the progress they'd made processing the scene. Shantel gave me permission to walk back and take a look at the body. Just then Dr. Darzi came walking up the drive with his two interns in tow.

We all walked back to look at Mrs. Baxter. She was as advertised—lying in her robe face down with an old, but well cared for, set of pruning shears buried to the hilt in her back. The entire back of her robe was soaked in blood. One of her slippers had come off when she fell. Her eyes were wide open and milky blue, staring toward the back gate. Looking at the scene, Maxwell's description of his actions seemed plausible.

I stepped forward and lifted her robe. She was wearing underwear that didn't appear to have been disturbed. As creepy as it seems, there are men who will sexually assault senior citizens.

"You always have such interesting deaths. When I retire and write my memoirs, I will be sure to give you credit," Dr. Darzi said.

"Thanks. We aim to please. If you can, give us a time of death and some idea of how much strength it would take to plunge those shears in that deep," I told him.

He nodded and moved over to the body to begin the formal examination. I left him to his morbid, but necessary, business to do a walk-through of the house.

Nothing inside seemed out of place. The house was neat and surprisingly uncluttered. I'd made some assumptions based on her age and sex, but there were only a couple of pictures and no knickknacks. There were several bookcases with quality editions of classic works of literature and a few more with nonfiction books covering a range of historical topics, from ancient Egypt to the Vietnam War.

All of the furniture was at least forty years old, but it looked brand new. She hadn't resorted to using plastic covers either. Judging from what Maxwell had said and what my eyes were telling me, it didn't look like the house had seen many other people since the old judge had died. The furniture had simply never been used because no one but Mrs. Baxter and a maid was ever in the house.

A spotless house was much easier to process than a messy one. We were also lucky that Mrs. Carrillo could tell us if anything was missing or had been moved. Under the you-have-to-consider-every-option rule, I had to consider the unlikely possibility that Mrs. Carrillo was involved. On the face of it, that seemed absurd, but crazier things have happened when it came to murder. Maybe a relative had killed Madge Baxter and Mrs. Carrillo was covering up for him, which would explain why she was so upset. It was a big pitfall for an investigator to start eliminating people based on preconceived notions.

By noon, the body was ready to be taken to Tallahassee. Seven o'clock was Dr. Darzi's approximate time of death, and he was pretty sure the cause of death was the large pair of pruning shears stuck through her back. Any other information would have to wait for the autopsy.

"You are spending so much time in our morgue, we'll have to put in a desk for you," Darzi joked on his way to the van.

"Not funny," I told him.

A couple of reporters were at the curb taking pictures and filming as the interns rolled the stretcher with Madge Baxter's body on it to the van. I went straight over to them, giving them a few basic facts and assuring them that I would text them any other details that I could before five o'clock so they could make the evening news.

After I'd seen the news folks off, I decided to canvass the neighbors. I was doing it not just because it needed to be done, and I might learn something that could help solve the case, but also to occupy my mind so that I didn't have to think about what I'd done at Pete's house that morning. What I'd done was a felony. Obstructing justice. How many people over the years had I warned about withholding evidence or information in a case? Now I found myself guilty of the same offense. I began to think that Dad had made a very bad decision by not turning the Harper murder over to state investigators.

The first house I visited was on the other side of Mrs. Baxter's. I didn't have to knock on the door, as a well dressed woman was sitting in the porch swing.

"I'm Deputy Larry Macklin," I said as I climbed the steps to the porch.

"I thought you were," she said. "I'm Nancy Bingham. I know your father." She did look familiar. I judged Ms. Bingham to be in her late fifties. She was broad shouldered and wore her pantsuit like a uniform.

"I'm sorry to tell you that your neighbor, Mrs. Baxter, has been killed," I told her.

She offered me a seat on one of the white wicker chairs that were strategically placed around the porch.

"I know. One of my friends called me. They heard enough on their police scanner to figure out what had happened. Do you know who's responsible?"

"We've just started our investigation. I wanted to ask you a few questions."

"Of course you do. But I don't think I'm going to be able

to help you much."

"Would you mind going over your movements this morning? Starting from the time you woke up."

"Sure. I woke up about seven-thirty. I retired last year and haven't been able to convince myself that I don't need to get up that early. I worked in the clerk's office down at the courthouse. That's where I got to know your father."

Something about the way she said that made me flash back to my morning run-in with Dad and Genie. Had he been flirting with other women around town and I'd just never noticed? I shuddered and tried to put that thought out of my mind.

"Did you hear anything out of the ordinary this morning? Particularly between six and eight."

"Was that when she was killed?" she asked with a hint of ghoulish interest.

"I'm sorry, but I can't give out any specific information on the case at this time."

"Oh, of course, I understand. No, I didn't hear anything out of the ordinary. Mr. Riley's dog was barking at one point, but that's not unusual. The dog usually finds a squirrel or two to bark at when he's let out to do his morning business."

"Did you notice what time the dog was barking?"

"Just as I was getting up, so about seven-thirty."

I made a mental note to talk with Mr. Riley about what his dog might have seen. "What did you do after you got up?"

"Just my usual. I got dressed, came downstairs and made coffee and oatmeal. I always check out the news on my laptop while I have breakfast, then my email and Facebook."

"Did you see or hear anything that stood out as unusual?"

"I heard Mrs. Carrillo yelling. Of course, I didn't know that's who it was at the time."

"What did you do?"

"I'm pretty nosy and nothing ever happens around here, so it piqued my curiosity. I went out on my porch and looked around, but I didn't see anything. I didn't know anything like… well, like a murder had happened until the police cars started showing up."

"Can you think of anyone who might have wanted to hurt Mrs. Baxter?"

"Ha, there's quite a few. She was not a person you could reason with. Very stubborn, and cheap. The man I use for odd jobs did some work for her once and ended up losing money."

"What's his name?"

"Oh, good lord. Hank wouldn't hurt a fly. He makes me look young," she said very convincingly. I let it drop for now. "Believe me, there are a lot of people who would be in line ahead of him."

"So give me your top ten list of suspects," I said conspiratorially, warming to her.

"Do you want a countdown or best first?" she asked, playing along.

"Best first," I said.

"Well, don't laugh, but I'd have to say Chief Maxwell." She wasn't kidding.

"Why do you put him at the top of the list?"

"He's the one who seemed to take her rejection of the alley project most personally. I saw him arguing with her once, and he balled up his fists. I honestly thought he might hit her."

As much as I disliked Maxwell, I still found it hard to envision him impaling an old woman with garden shears. "Okay, number two?"

"Her sister. She lives in Savannah, so she might have an alibi, but there was no love lost between them. When their daddy died back around 1990, there was a lot of paperwork that had to be done with the estate. I saw them together a couple of times at the courthouse, and if hate had mass, they both would have fallen into the center of the Earth. Of course, I'd heard Madge talk about her sister for years and every word was venomous. From what others said, the disdain was mutual."

"Third?"

"There was a man who replaced her roof about two years ago. He threatened her a couple of times. Yelling loud enough on her front lawn for me to hear him inside the house. Apparently, she had tricked him into doing a lot of the work without paying him. She nitpicked him over a million little things, like the Chinese torture of death by a thousand cuts. Madge took him to court two or three times until he just gave up."

"Do you have his name?"

"I can probably find it."

I pulled out my card and handed it to her. "Call me when you have it. Fourth?"

We went through the rest of her list, which degenerated fairly quickly into a number of small arguments and petty fights. As I left, I reminded her to call me with the roofer's name.

Mr. Riley and his dog were next on my list, but he wasn't home. Another neighbor told me that he worked for a law firm with an office on the courthouse square. I checked in with Shantel and Marcus, who were close to wrapping up, then headed out to find Mr. Riley.

CHAPTER NINE

After driving around the square, I found the offices of Riley & Dodge Real Estate Attorneys tucked away between a yoga studio and a dentist. I was always amazed when I noticed something for the first time that I must have passed a hundred times. The offices had obviously been there for years, but I couldn't remember ever having seen them.

Inside, a very attractive young woman sat at the reception desk. I noticed that her last name was Dodge and figured her for the partner's daughter.

"Can I help you?" she asked brightly.

"I'd like to talk with Mr. Riley," I said, showing her my badge.

"Which case does this pertain to?" She clicked her computer mouse and looked at the monitor.

"Not a case he's working on," I said, causing her to look up at me. I decided not to mess with her and explained, "One of Mr. Riley's neighbor's died this morning and I need to ask him a few questions."

Her eyes got big. "I see," she said, trying to maintain her composure. "Let me just check and see if he's available."

Probably not wanting me to hear, she got up and went to his office rather than buzzing him on the house phone. She was gone for about five minutes. When she came back, she gave me a little smile and told me I could go in.

Mr. Riley's office was far from impressive. The walls were covered in seventies-era wood paneling, while the carpet looked like it had been there since the day that Richard Nixon resigned. Mr. Riley was a serious-looking man in an off-the-rack coat. He stood up behind a wooden desk that could have come from any government office twenty years ago.

"Will Riley," he said, reaching over the desk to shake my hand. "How can I help you? Linda said that one of my neighbors has died?" His brow was furrowed with concern.

"I'm afraid that Mrs. Baxter died this morning." I was a bit surprised that he hadn't heard about the murder. Hadn't any of his neighbors or friends called him?

"I'm sorry to hear that," he said, looking almost like he meant it. "I assume that there is more to it than a natural death. Otherwise you wouldn't be here."

"You're right. I can tell you that she was killed." I watched his face for any reaction. He just blinked at me.

"Really."

"I would like to ask you a few questions about your morning."

"Am I under suspicion?" he said, trying to make it sound light, but underneath I could hear the seriousness of his question.

"Why do you ask? Should you be?" I tossed back at him.

"Well, no. Sorry, I was trying to make a joke. Guess it's in rather bad taste. But, seriously, as a former defense lawyer, I always have to question the motives of law enforcement."

"I can honestly say that the only reason I'm here now is due to the fact that you live directly behind the victim. You'll know when I consider you a person of interest." I meant the last part as a joke, but like his, the humor was lost.

He frowned a little, but at last nodded in agreement. "I'll be glad to answer any questions I can."

"Start with when you woke up this morning and tell me

what you did after that."

"Not much to tell. I got up at sixty-thirty, took a quick shower and then let Skyler out in the backyard while I fixed breakfast. I ate and got dressed for work. Let Skyler back in and left for work about eight."

"Did you see or hear anything unusual?"

"Ahhh, not really," he said, squinting his eyes in thought.

"One of your neighbors mentioned that they heard your dog barking," I said and he smiled ruefully.

"Skyler. He's got some Bluetick in him. Loves to tree anything that can climb and then sit there and bark at it. If I have to get up especially early, I go out and stand with him so he doesn't get to barking too much and wake all the neighbors. I try to be a responsible member of the community. You know, though, it's funny that you mention him barking this morning. He sounded a little different than he normally does."

"How so?"

"I guess 'cause he wasn't looking up into one of the pecan trees and barking like usual. Instead he was barking at the privacy fence."

"Does that fence separate your property from the alley?"

"The alley." He rolled his eyes upward. "Let's not get started on the alley. But, yes, I am talking about the fence across my backyard. I went to let him inside and saw him staring through the fence. It's in pretty bad shape, but what with all the talk about us taking over our part of the alley, I haven't seen the point of replacing it."

"Do you think he could have been barking at someone in the alley?"

"Oh, yeah. That could certainly be what he was doing. Anytime he's in the yard and there's someone in the alley, he'll bark at them." He was looking very thoughtful.

"Is there something else you remember?"

"Well, now that you've brought it up, I think there *was* someone in the alley. Like I said, the fence isn't in very good shape so I can kind of see through it. And when I was calling

Skyler, I thought I saw something moving out there. Didn't really see much, though."

"What time was this?"

"I guess around seven-thirty." Dr. Darzi had given a rough estimate of seven, but this was still well within the margin of error.

"Could you tell which way the person might have been going?"

He shook his head. "Skyler was moving back and forth along the fence, so it's hard to say. If I had to guess, I'd say away from the gate in Mrs. Baxter's fence. But that's only a guess."

"Do you know of anyone who might have held a grudge against Madge Baxter? Or was angry with her about something?"

He smiled. "Am I the first person you've interviewed?"

"No."

"Then I'm sure that you've already had an earful about all the people she's had run-ins with. I doubt that I could add anything. Have you heard about the alley situation?"

I nodded.

"Well, I was asked to help with the legal issues since real estate law is my specialty. I would have been glad to help, but as soon as I heard that Madge was against it, I told Maxwell that I didn't want to have anything to do with it. I would support it if everyone was on board, but no way was I going to get into a fight with Madge. She was willing to take every fight down to the mat. I didn't need a mortal enemy living two hundred feet from where I sleep."

"Was she that bad?"

"Oh, yeah. Must have been twenty years ago when I first moved in, she found out I was a lawyer and asked me to help out because a contractor was trying to cheat her out of some money. I thought I'd be nice and help the senior citizen. But I found out soon enough that it was the contractor who needed defending. I managed to work it out, but the solution involved me helping the contractor get a big job with a friend of mine to help him recover a bit financially. I told myself I'd never have any business dealings with her again." He shuddered. "Guess I shouldn't talk ill of the dead."

I tried a few more times to get him to name names, but he was determined not to point fingers. I thanked him for his time and left.

I had a late lunch at a taco stand that had popped up in the last month. Adams County's Hispanic population had grown over the last decade, with many who came to work in the tomato fields deciding to stay and put down roots. One of our old mom-and-pop grocery stores was now a mom-and-pop mercado.

The tacos and chips were good, and the smile and kind eyes of the woman working the counter was a tonic for the anxiety I felt over the recent murders.

I called Darlene and asked her how things were going with the Todd Harper investigation. I heard a moment's hesitation on her end of the phone.

"This is a mess and then some. I'm not sure whether you're on the case or not," she said. "And don't you dare tell me anything about the Baxter murder."

"I'm not going to, but I just might need to question you. You know Maxwell pretty well, and you might be able to give me some insight into his motivations and actions."

"You have a point."

"Let's meet at the office this afternoon. There isn't too much more that I can do until the autopsy's done and we go through the evidence. It's a good time to talk. I can't slip up and tell you too much because, right now, I don't know much that won't be in the papers tomorrow."

"Okay, three o'clock."

I had an hour to kill. I spent most of it trying to figure out what to do with the piece of evidence from Pete's house. I needed to get it processed, but telling anyone else about it would either land me in prison or put them in a situation similar to mine. With no good option coming immediately to mind, I did the only thing I could think of. I went to the bank and rented a safe deposit box. I put the evidence bag containing the knob into the box, along with a detailed note explaining how and when it had been collected. Then I sealed the key in an envelope and slipped it into my pocket.

I got to the office a few minutes after three and went straight to the conference room. As I was texting Darlene to tell her where I was, she walked in the door.

"I'm going to record our conversation," I said.

"Makes sense. Don't want anyone thinking we're colluding on the Baxter murder."

"Though I don't really know how that's any different than me being involved in the Harper investigation. Maxwell's no better a friend to you than Pete is to me."

"Has your dad called for the state to oversee the Baxter murder?"

"Not yet. I don't think he realizes that Maxwell is at the top of everyone's list for offing the old woman."

"The other difference between the two cases is that your dad probably trusts you a bit more than me. I've only worked for the department for a couple of months, while I worked under Maxwell for years."

Her mentioning the trust that Dad was placing in me with the Harper case made me realize how devastated he would be if he found out I was obstructing justice to protect Pete. I made a quick decision and took the envelope out of my pocket, handing it across the table to Darlene.

"What's this?"

"Will you hold onto this for me? If something was to happen to me, I'd want you to open it."

She squinted, obviously curious what this was all about. "Is this some kind of trust game? 'Cause I'm rotten at them. I might open it up two minutes after I leave the room."

I didn't believe it for a minute. By giving her the key to the safe deposit box, she would be a witness to the latest point at which the knob of the bat could have been placed there. If I had wildly miscalculated the situation and something did happen to me, I knew that Darlene would open the box and make a professional judgment about what to do with it. And if I figured out some way to have it tested, or decided that it needed to be turned over as evidence, I could take Darlene with me to the bank to open the box and turn it over to her. Of course, after reading the note I enclosed with it, she'd have very little choice but to handcuff me and read me my rights. *Let's hope it doesn't come to that*, I thought.

"I'll take my chances," I told her.

"Your funeral," she said with a small upturn at the corners of her mouth as she stuffed the envelope into her pocket.

"Down to the nitty-gritty. Have you ever seen Maxwell lose his temper?"

"I've seen him very angry. But I've never seen him strike out at anyone. If someone embarrasses him or says something personally insulting, he can become verbally abusive. But even then, I've always seen him keep it under control. He also doesn't tolerate incompetence from his employees. His commitment to excellence was one of the things I liked about working for him. I saw it in him when he spoke to my academy class. That's why I applied in Calhoun. However, his expectations are sometimes... I'd say unreasonable. Not everyone can give one hundred percent one hundred percent of the time, especially at the pay scale of a small city police department."

"Why do you think he hasn't moved up before now?" Now being his run for sheriff against Dad.

"Where would he go? His wife has a very good position at FSU and he's absolutely devoted to her. Considering that he can be a stuck-up jerk, his affection for his wife is endearing. So, the answer to your question is that they came up here for her career, and he wanted to be the boss wherever he worked. That ruled out taking a job with any of the law enforcement organizations in Tallahassee. And he couldn't run for sheriff of Adams County until he'd established himself as a member of the community. So here we are."

"How much do you know about his feud with Madge Baxter?"

"Just what's known publicly. I was at the city commission meeting where they got into a shouting match."

"What exactly happened?"

"You can see a lot of it for yourself. They record all the meetings and post them on the city's website. But the CliffsNotes version is that Maxwell asked the commission to give a preliminary okay to turning the alley over to the owners of the adjoining properties. When one of the commissioners asked if all the property owners were in agreement about the move, Maxwell said that he had talked to all of them and that they were *going* to be in agreement. Obviously, he was fudging the answer.

"I don't know if he knew that Madge was at the meeting or not. He was sitting in the front while she came in late and sat in the back row. Anyway, when he said that, she stood up and yelled that he was a liar. I swear, you can see his face turn red in the video. He wheeled around and told her to shut up and sit down, which infuriated Madge, who began making her way toward the front of the room. The chairwoman tried to gavel the meeting back to order while half the crowd was laughing and enjoying seeing the chief of police taken down a peg by a crazy old woman. Crazy old woman is how most of the town saw Madge. Probably anyone who'd ever had business dealings with her was hoping that Maxwell would put her in chains and drag her off to jail."

"So what you're saying is that half the crowd was rooting for Madge and half was rooting for the chief?"

"Actually, if was more that half was rooting against the chief and half was rooting against Madge."

"How did it end?"

"With the sergeant-at-arms escorting Madge out of the meeting to a rumble of boos."

"Did Maxwell overtly threaten her?"

"No, he mostly riffed on the theme of her being crazy."

"Do you know if they had any other altercations?"

"You can check the reports. He did claim that she harassed him about a month after the commission meeting. That she was calling him up and yelling obscenities at him. I don't doubt it, as we had taken reports from a couple of neighbors that were receiving unwanted calls from her. She would beg them not to go along with the alley project and when they said anything positive about it, she'd start shouting and calling them names. Nothing new. We'd received reports like this from people who had worked for her for years. She would decide what was right and then fight tooth and nail against anyone and everyone who dared to think differently."

I asked a couple more questions, but Darlene didn't have much more to add. I started to get up, but she stopped me.

"I've been thinking... I don't know about you, but I could use all the help I can get on the Harper case."

"You're better off than me. Lt. Johnson's just about the only person I can discuss my case with."

"I don't think that FDLE is going to be able to give us a lot of assistance."

"No. Especially since we aren't asking them to come in and take over."

"Exactly." Uncharacteristically, she seemed hesitant to talk.

"What's on your mind?"

"There's a guy in town. His name's Edward Landon. I've met him a couple of times. He's a retired criminologist. He's taught at several universities, and given seminars and helped out a number of law enforcement agencies. Anyway, I ran into him yesterday evening and we got to talking."

She saw my face and said, "No, nothing about the Harper case. Just talked about his work, and he mentioned he was looking to do some consulting. This morning I got to thinking that we could use an outsider on both of these cases to give us a little perspective."

She had a point. I sat back in my chair and tried to map out all the angles. "The biggest problem would probably be money," I said. "As long as his background checked out."

"Money, yeah. I know he's who he says he is because the first time I met him was when Maxwell sent me to Quantico for some training. He didn't teach the class, but he did present a case to us." *She got to go to Quantico?* I thought, regretting, not for the first time, that I'd blown my one chance to go by choosing to attend Shot Show in Vegas instead.

"Why did he retire here? Is he from the Tallahassee area?"

"He's not, but his parents live down in Panama City now and he wanted to be close enough to them to help them out as they got older. He thought that, by being near the capital, he might be able to get some consulting work with the state. He's only been living here about six months."

"Interesting. I'll ask Dad what he thinks. I don't think it would hurt to approach him."

"Your dad or the consultant?"

"Both. Maybe he'll give us a hometown discount." I looked at my watch and saw that it was almost four. "I'll go see if Dad's here. If so, I'll see if I can get the okay to at least talk to the guy."

CHAPTER TEN

Dad was in his office. Mauser got up and came over to lean against me, begging for an ear rub. I hated to admit it, but a little dog therapy was welcome.

"Sit down," Dad said to me after Mauser got tired of standing up and went back to his bed.

"Life sucks," I said.

"You've got that right," Dad said, sounding glum. I really preferred to see him in a fighting mood.

"Darlene had a suggestion…" I proceeded to tell him about the consultant.

"I've got some contacts. I'll check up on him. It's better than using a psychic, I guess. We'd have to work out the budget, and I'd want an ironclad confidentiality contract. I'd want to be able to put him in jail and sue his ass if he leaked anything." The fact that he hadn't immediately shot the idea down was a testament to how concerned he was about these cases. "Then again, we might be getting ahead of ourselves. Both of the investigations are still young. None of the lab results are back. Hell, Mrs. Baxter's body is still warm."

"This is more about clearing Pete and Maxwell," I said.

"I know. The longer this goes on, the more heat we're going to come under. And I hate to admit it, but this will probably reduce the effectiveness of the Calhoun Police Department when we're already stretched and could use their help. Plus, I don't need anyone suggesting that I'm leaving Maxwell on the hot seat for political reasons."

"Is it possible that we're talking about one killer?" I asked, an idea just beginning to take shape.

Dad looked thoughtful. "Motive is the problem. What would be the motive? Wait, stop. I really don't want to discuss the Baxter case."

"And that's why having a consultant to bounce ideas off of would help."

"I see your point. FDLE will send someone over here in a couple of weeks to assess our progress and procedures on the Harper case."

"We don't know who they'll send or how much time they will actually be able to devote to it. And two weeks is too damn long."

"True. Okay, let me check this consultant's background," he said, his tone suggesting that he was done with me. I got up and started toward the door.

"Oh, yeah, one more thing."

I turned and looked at him, knowing that nothing good was coming.

"Genie and I are going down to Orlando this weekend. I'd cancel the trip with everything going on, but the whole reason I'm going is to lead a training seminar on rural community law enforcement for the sheriff's association. As it is, I'm going to cut it short and come back on Saturday evening." He stopped because we both knew what was implied.

"Let me guess. Jamie's busy."

"His mother is sick and he needs to help out his dad. If you could just feed the horses on Friday and Saturday. We won't get back until late. And, if you don't mind, keep Mauser from Friday until Sunday morning."

I looked over at the black-and-white monster lying on the twin mattress that Dad had made up for him. He looked back at me with his big brown eyes as if to say, *Please, I'll be good*, though it was almost certainly not true.

"Sure. It's not like I have anything else to do," I said sarcastically.

"That's what I thought," Dad lobbed back. And then, as I turned toward the door again, he surprised me by saying, "Thanks."

I lifted my hand in a backward acknowledgement. At least having Mauser around would provide a distraction from the chaos that seemed to be swirling around me. Or it might just add to it.

I went home to a quiet evening. Cara was going in early to the vet on Wednesday to help with the dog walking and to prep for surgeries. Since she'd have to be there by seven, she had decided to stay at her own place. Ivy seemed very happy to have me to herself for a change as I watched a little TV and then called it an early night.

The next morning, I got in before eight and started tackling my reports on both murders. Dr. Darzi texted me that the Baxter autopsy was scheduled for two o'clock. At eleven, Darlene came over to my desk and told me that she'd tracked down Samuel Ellison through his parole officer.

"I had his parole officer contact Ellison and set up a meeting at noon when Ellison takes his lunch break. He works at Walmart on the east side of Tallahassee. If you can make it, I'd appreciate the backup."

"That actually works for me. We can take separate cars. I've got the Baxter autopsy at two. But I'm not actually on the Harper investigation anymore."

Considering that I had already tampered with evidence, I wasn't sure if I wanted to be more involved in the case. Part of my mind was in complete denial, hoping that if I just gave it a couple of days, Darlene would solve the case and life could return to normal.

"Doesn't mean you can't be present for an interview. This guy sounds like a piece of work. Pretty savvy on how the system works. I'd wouldn't mind you being present."

"No problem."

She looked at me quizzically. After I'd given her the envelope and now seemed hesitant to be involved in the case, she must have wondered what was up with me.

"I *do* want to be kept up on the Harper case," I said lamely, which probably sounded even more odd. I was violating a key rule: *If you are in a hole, the first thing to do is stop digging.*

"Okay. Good."

We parked next to each other at the Walmart and Darlene went inside to get Ellison. From his priors he didn't deserve it, but we figured we'd be nice and not look too much like a couple of cops coming to get him at his job.

I stood by the car enjoying a moment in the sunshine and the spring breeze. After a few minutes, Darlene and Ellison came walking toward me. Everything about him screamed ex-con, from the homemade tattoos on his neck and hands to the cold eyes that stared right through me.

"Mr. Ellison, this is Deputy Macklin," Darlene said to him when they were within ten feet of me. "I told him we'd buy him a sandwich."

We all climbed into Darlene's car and, five minutes later, pulled into the parking lot of a Wendy's.

"It's not very private," Darlene told him.

"Like I give a shit," Ellison said. "I don't want to eat in the damn car."

We got our food and sat down at a booth. I made sure that we weren't near any kids. I really didn't think the conversation was going to be the type to lead to sweet dreams.

"What's this about?" Ellison asked with a mouth full of chicken sandwich.

"We're investigating the murder of a man named Todd Harper," Darlene told him.

"Never heard of him. But thanks for the meal," he said, grabbing a dozen fries and cramming them into his mouth.

"You claim not to know Todd Harper?"

"That's right. Got a picture?" he asked snidely.

"Actually, I do." Darlene picked up her phone from the table and pulled up a picture of Todd, showing it to Ellison. When he saw the image he almost spat out the fries. "From your expression, can I assume that you remember him?"

"I'd like to kill…" He realized what he was mumbling and looked up at us. "Yeah, I ain't sorry at all to hear he's dead. I hope it was painful as shit." He went back to the sandwich.

"Where were you on Saturday night and Sunday morning?" Darlene pressed him.

"At home. Guess you know where that is. I heard you'd come by," he snarled.

"Anybody there with you?"

"Yeah, the Pope and Madonna. No, there wasn't anyone there."

"We'd like to look around your apartment."

"What'cha asking me for? I'm on parole. You can do whatever the hell you want," he said, looking down at his food. He was eating slower. Maybe the questions were spoiling his appetite. "You got my DNA, my fingerprints. Hell, you probably got bottles of my piss somewhere. I'm done talking."

"You know, that's not a good attitude. What you did to that woman was a crime, and we are well within the statute of limitations for assault and battery and attempted sexual assault. I could probably think of a couple of other charges."

"What about what they did to me?" he argued in the best tradition of the downtrodden criminal. "'Sides, now it's just her word against mine," he continued, obviously not thinking about the fact that he was giving us a very good motive for murder. Darlene helpfully pointed that out to him.

"That's the second motive you have for killing Mr. Harper. The first is revenge."

"What do you want me to say? I was at home. You know

I'd like to have killed him, but I didn't even know the pissant's name, let alone where he lived."

"How'd you know he was killed at home?" Darlene zeroed in on his comment.

"I didn't. I just meant I wouldn't know where to find him if I'd wanted to."

"You just said you wanted to."

"The hell with you people. I want to get back to work. Search my apartment, check my damn DNA, do whatever you want. I didn't do anything to him." He stood up and started stomping toward the door.

We drove him back to the Walmart where I got my car.

"Guess I've got my work cut out for me," Darlene said. She'd already called Ellison's parole officer and arranged to meet him at Ellison's apartment.

"Good hunting," I told her. "I'm off to the morgue for another autopsy."

"Lucky you," she said. She paused a moment, as if she wanted to ask me a question but wasn't sure if she wanted the answer. But instead of saying anything, she just got in her car and drove off, leaving me feeling more isolated than ever.

The autopsy would have been comical if we hadn't been dealing with someone who had once lived and breathed. No amount of professionalism could make moving a body with pruning shears sticking a foot out of the back of it anything but awkward, like a scene from a morbid and long-lost Three Stooges movie.

Darzi and his team managed to work around them. After the body was measured and probed, it was time to pull the shears from the body. They were wedged through the muscles of the back and into the ribcage. It took Darzi and an intern both to separate them from Mrs. Baxter.

"Took a lot of strength to ram them through the back like that. The killer had to have been physically strong," Darzi told me.

"How strong? Like normal-adult-male strong or Arnold-Schwarzenegger-in-his-prime strong?"

"An adult who has spent some time working out. Maybe has had some training." Maxwell easily fit that mold.

Darzi took the tray with the shears and handed it over to his assistant, who left the room with them.

"I know that your crime scene people went over the handles for fingerprints and trace evidence before we moved the body. We'll see if we can find anything else. You should have your own Black Museum," Darzi said, alluding to Scotland Yard's famous repository of ghoulish artifacts.

After Darzi finished with his initial examination, he told me that it appeared that the murderer simply came up behind Mrs. Baxter and cold-bloodedly rammed the shears through her back.

"She twisted a little bit back and forth on the blades, but some of that movement can be attributed to her body going limp and hanging momentarily on the weapon before the killer let go of the shears."

With that last horrible image on my mind, I left Dr. Darzi and his assistants to finish taking tissue samples and weighing the organs.

Driving home that evening, I reflected on the last couple of days. Something about the murders seemed off to me. There was zero proof that there was a connection between them, but now that the idea was in my head, I was having a hard time shaking it.

Cara, Alvin and Ivy were waiting for me when I got home.

"Listen up, everyone. We're going to have company this weekend. Mauser the canine bulldozer is coming for a sleepover."

"Why are we being honored with his presence?" Cara asked, and I explained about Dad's trip to Orlando.

"He and Genie are getting to be the real deal." I rolled my eyes a bit and she laughed. "Don't be a wet blanket. It's good for your dad to have someone."

"I know. And she's all right. Actually, he probably needs

to get away for a day. Being the control freak that he is, it must be driving him crazy to have two cases that he can't or shouldn't be involved in."

We settled down on the couch after dinner. Instead of immediately turning on the TV, I asked Cara to tell me all about her day.

"Why do you want to hear about cleaning up doggy accidents and pulling cats off of my head?"

"Because it's completely removed from the sheriff's office, the morgue and dead bodies."

"Okay, you asked for it." She proceeded to talk about all the latest developments at the clinic, including a new tech who wasn't very good with cats, a client that couldn't seem to keep her dog on a diet and a possible romance between the receptionist and a particularly handsome owner of an English Bulldog.

The non-murder related news was a nice break for my mind, but as soon as Cara finished and leaned back in the couch, all of my dark thoughts came rushing back.

"What's wrong?" Cara must have seen it in my face. "I know that the situation with Pete is worrying you."

"It's not just that. It's also that Pete's problem doesn't allow us to work together. Darlene is good, but I count on Pete as a sounding board. I can't... shouldn't discuss anything with him. And now, with the Baxter murder, I also have to watch what I say around Darlene." I had a sudden desire to unburden myself on Cara, but I was hesitant to transfer any of the weight to her shoulders.

"You can tell me anything. I know that you aren't supposed to talk to me about a lot of stuff, but you know you can trust me."

She pushed a little and I caved. My excuse to myself was that I was tired, but I really just needed to confess.

"There is something. And I'm not proud of what I've done." At this point I realized that I would have to tell her the whole story, but I wanted her to have a choice. Even if in reality it was no choice at all.

"I want to know everything about you. I promise I won't judge you," she said solemnly.

"Others would judge me, and harshly," I said and went on to tell her what Pete had found and what we did.

"Wow," she said softly, looking a little dazed. "Just… wow. Does all that mean what I think it means?"

"Probably. I hid evidence. That's a felony. Pete is also guilty. And if this ever comes out, my dad will be crushed. He may not think much of me as an investigator, but I know that he respects Pete."

"Was there any other choice?"

"Several. But right at that moment, with the clock ticking, we didn't come up with one. Now we're stuck. This isn't an error that you can just undo."

"You could always put it back in the grill."

"We could. But odds are that the truth would come out. There are records of where we were and when. I've gotten paranoid now and I don't even want to call him and ask how he's doing. It's crazy."

"You were just caught up in the moment."

"You can't tell the arresting officer or the judge that. They won't care. Dad won't care. The more time passes and the more I think about it, the more convinced I am that we are well and truly screwed."

"Then you just have to find the real killer," Cara said with conviction.

"Easier said than done. Especially since I'm not really even supposed to be working that case. I have my own high-profile murder investigation to deal with."

"Darlene is good. You've said that."

"She *is* good. Probably better than me. But even a great investigator can run up against a brick wall. And the irony is that I'm handicapping her by withholding evidence. To top it all off, I think the pressure is screwing up my mind."

"I doubt that." Cara had settled into full nurturing mode.

"I don't. I've gotten it into my head that the two cases are linked somehow, which doesn't make any sense. There isn't any evidence to even suggest there's a connection."

"Why would you think they're linked if they aren't?"

"Probably wishful thinking. If they're linked, then by solving one we'd solve the other."

"There must be something. I don't think you're going crazy."

"I see some similarities, but I think they're just coincidences. Like how, in both cases, the killer seems oddly disengaged from the murders," I said vaguely.

"What do you mean?"

"In the first case, the attack looked pretty severe. He'd been hit more than once with a baseball bat. But when you analyze it, you realize that he wasn't hit any more times than you'd need to make sure that the job got done. And the only hits were to the head. If someone was murdering a person that they hated, they'd most likely go to town on the victim, even after they were down on the ground. I'd expect to see damage to his arms, ribs, maybe even his thighs, legs and groin. So no anger was exhibited. The killer was ruthless, but not angry.

"Same with the second murder. The killer just came up behind her and rammed the shears through her back. Very business-like. It's the sort of thing I'd expect from a person who wanted someone out of the way so they'd inherit, get their girlfriend or get their job. Something like that."

"Mrs. Baxter was pretty rich, wasn't she? Maybe that murder *was* for an inheritance."

"Maybe. We're still in the process of getting all her bank records. I talked to her attorney and we're going to meet tomorrow. He said that several different groups will inherit the bulk of the estate, but that the estate isn't anywhere near as large as one would have thought."

"Look at the lawyer. Maybe he was embezzling funds."

"Trust me, we'll follow the money trail wherever it leads. One of our investigators, Lucas—I don't think you've met him—is wicked with numbers. I'll get him to go over her accounts. But what about Harper? His family may have money, but by all appearances he was just scraping by."

"Maybe he had some trust fund that he was going to inherit, and he was killed before he could get it."

"His mother didn't mention it."

"I hate to say it, but if a father was scared that a boy might hurt his daughter, couldn't he take a clinical approach to getting rid of him?"

"That thought has crossed my mind. And we've both seen Pete at the range. He can be very cool and calculating. But if Pete was going to go about it in a cold-blooded, planned manner, he'd do it right. He wouldn't do it after he'd just blown up at the kid in front of God and everybody."

"Pete's not stupid."

"And he cares deeply about his family, and he knows that they care deeply about him. So he wouldn't do anything to endanger that relationship. Unfortunately, that argument will get you exactly nowhere with a state attorney, judge or jury. Smart people do dumb things all the time. Usually people chalk it up to arrogance. The killer, because he's smart, thinks he can get away with it. The only way to remove the cloud that's hanging over Pete is to find out who really did it." I paused and took her hand. "You realize that by telling you about the piece of the bat, I've made you an accessory?"

"I know that," Cara said, chewing on her lower lip thoughtfully.

"I'd advise you to call the sheriff's office or the State Attorney the first chance you get and tell them everything you know." I said this sincerely. It flitted through my head that maybe that's why I'd told her.

"I don't think I'll do that. I trust you and Pete. We'll get through this," she said, squeezing my hand tightly.

Her confidence made me feel better, but I just hoped that it wasn't misplaced.

CHAPTER ELEVEN

I didn't sleep well, wondering what was wrong with my judgment lately. I woke up feeling as tired as when I'd gone to bed. I could hear Cara taking a shower and Alvin eating his breakfast in the kitchen. Ivy was standing on top of me, staring into my eyes accusingly. Was it because she knew that my rash decisions were putting her cushy life in danger, or was it only that she wanted me to hurry up and get my cereal so she could drink some of the milk? Hard to tell.

I left Cara texting with Pete, planning their schedule to meet out at the range. She had promised to tell him that I'd be in touch when I could, and she also swore *not* to tell him that she knew about the piece of baseball bat.

My phone started ringing before I'd managed to get my car started.

"Is this Deputy Macklin?" asked a voice with a serious Texas drawl.

"Yep, who is this?"

"Steve Winter. I'm a retired Texas Ranger. I've been hired by the family of Todd Harper to look into his murder."

Every muscle in my body clenched up. A private eye muddying the waters was just what we didn't need.

"Mr. Winter, as a former law enforcement officer, you'll

understand that this case is still very new, so we are not about to give out much information." I tried to sound as self-assured as he did.

"And, as a former law enforcement officer, I realize that even the best departments make mistakes. I'm here on behalf of my clients to make sure that doesn't happen in Todd's case."

I made the decision to pass on this particular hot potato. "I'm actually not the lead investigator on the Harper case; Deputy Darlene Marks is. I suggest that you discuss your concerns with her. But I don't think you'll have much luck." I threw in the last line just to stir the pot.

"I'll do that. But don't be surprised if you and I have some business to discuss," he said cryptically and disconnected.

What the hell was that? A threat? I thought, looking at the phone and putting his name in my contacts. I wanted his ID to pop up if he called again.

When I got to my desk, I saw Darlene standing nearby, talking on the phone. Her face was pinched into a very ugly expression and her hand was resting on the butt of her gun. I was pretty sure I knew who she was talking to.

"I'll be damned!" she growled, punching at her phone's screen. "I'm not going to have some jacked-up cowboy coming in on a case I'm working and fu… screw it up." I wasn't sure if she was talking to me or to herself.

"He called me first," I told her.

"Not surprised. Probably a misogynistic bastard too." It was clear that Mr. Winter had managed to burrow under her skin. Darlene visibly shook herself to calm down.

I told her that Dad was still thinking about the consultant.

"I hope he goes for it. I wouldn't mind the help."

"Same here." I also thought about suggesting the possibility that the two cases might be connected, but decided that would involve giving her too many details about the Baxter case.

I spent most of the day following up on the Baxter case. Madge hadn't bothered with a password on her phone, so it had only taken IT a minute to transfer all of the information to a data file that I could look at on my laptop. Nothing jumped out. The number that she texted and called most often was that of her lawyer. I also found her sister's number. The last time they had talked was at Christmas. I decided to give her a call.

"Her lawyer already contacted me," Sylvia Harris told me, sounding irritated.

"Were you planning on coming to Calhoun?"

"Not if I can help it. Madge's instructions for her estate are that everything, and the lawyer emphasized everything, is to be sold. If I want anything of sentimental value, then I have to bid on it. Have you ever heard of anything so... mean? And I mean that in both definitions of the word."

"What happens to the proceeds of the sale?"

"Ha! It's to be divided up. Some will go to the local historical society, which she never gave a crap about, but apparently they sided with her on some lawsuit she filed. The Methodist church will get some, maybe because she's trying to buy her way into heaven and good luck with that. And, finally, she included the Libertarian Party of Florida, for who the hell knows why. She was as crazy as she was hateful, which is saying something."

"Did you know about the will's beneficiaries before her death?"

"I knew she wasn't going to give me—or anyone else in my family—anything, if that's what you mean. Mad Madge made that clear years ago. And if you're wondering if I had a motive to kill her, let me tell you that profit wouldn't have been it. I've got a million slights, slaps and insults that would have given me more than enough reason to kill that—

"No, I'm done calling her names. She was my sister. We never got along. I reached out time and time again to her and, every time, she bit my hand. But I'm going to use her death as a way to let go of all that hate. Oh, by the way, I can prove that I was here in Savannah when she was killed. Also, trust me, if I was going to send her to the hereafter, I would have done it with my own two hands." She took a deep breath. "I'm now letting go of the hate. Letting go," Sylvia chanted with the calming tones of a yoga instructor.

"Do you know of anyone else who might have wanted her dead?"

"From our childhood on up until the 1990s, I can write up a couple pages of names. For the last two decades, I haven't spent any time with her. I'm sure there are plenty of folks who live down there who can make a list for you. Look, seriously, she was a wicked woman, but most of the things she did were just petty little crap that a normal person gets over. Most people never got close enough to her to be murderously angry with her."

She gave me contact information for the people in Savannah who could vouch for her whereabouts and also the names of a few people who might have more information about Madge's recent activities.

Madge's lawyer had agreed to meet with me over lunch. His office was in downtown Tallahassee, so he invited me to the exclusive Governor's Club, a favorite watering hole of the capital city's lawyers, lobbyists and legislators.

Daniel Maitland was already sitting at a table when I arrived. "Hope you don't mind. I went ahead and ordered a drink. I don't usually do the *Mad Men* thing, but it's been one of those days," he said after we'd introduced ourselves.

Once we'd placed our orders, Maitland said, "I can't believe that someone actually killed Madge Baxter. Of course, with the number of enemies that she collected, you're probably not hurting for suspects. Madge was one of the most unlikable people I've ever had to deal with. I honestly wondered if it was some form of mental illness. I can tell you she might have benefited from a medical marijuana law. If you could have gotten her to take it, maybe it would have mellowed her out a little. Couldn't have hurt." He took a drink of what looked like a Long Island Iced Tea.

"I spoke with her sister. She said the will says to sell everything."

"Yep. Pretty cruel to her sister. I asked Madge, carefully of course, if there was bad blood between them. Madge just said that Sylvia didn't need the money. I didn't press it."

"Do you know of any individual who would benefit from the will?"

"Oh, like someone working at the church or something? I don't think that anyone except Madge and me knew about the contents of the will. She always played her cards close to her chest. Hell, I think she hated the fact that I *had* to know some of her business. Honestly, I expected the day would come when she'd try to sue me. Madge litigated every bill she ever got. I think she considered it part of the bargaining process. First you get an estimate, then you bargain them down, you agree on a price, they do the work and then you sue them, hoping to knock down the price a little more."

"How long have you been her lawyer?"

"Since before her husband died. I worked for a bigger firm that Judge Baxter used. He was a criminal lawyer before becoming a judge, and he was the kind of guy who was smart enough to know that he wasn't an expert in everything. I was young, and Baxter, who was the exact opposite of Madge, was kind enough to let me work on his account, mostly business transactions. When he died, Madge just kept using me. I think it was the connection with her husband that kept her from abusing me like she did everyone else. He was the only person in the world that she actually seemed to care about."

"Was there anyone that you would say was particularly upset with Mrs. Baxter?"

"You might not like me saying this, but Chief Maxwell was really very aggressive with her. He seemed a bit less willing to chalk her attitude up to her being a grumpy old lady. I'm sure that he just wanted to get the alley situation settled. Of course, it *was* settled. She was never going to change her mind. Maxwell just didn't like taking no for an answer."

"I can imagine."

I asked him about a few of the other individuals that Ms. Bingham had mentioned, including the roofer, then enjoyed spending the rest of lunch listening to various stories about Madge.

As I was walking back to my car, I got a text from Dad: *Consultant seems legit. If he keeps his charges under fifty dollars an hour, go for it. Max of twenty-five hundred.* I called Darlene with the news and she said she'd get in contact with Landon. By the time I got back to the office, he had agreed to meet with us at his house at four. We both went to our desks and put together a dossier on our cases for him.

Cara called as she was leaving the range. "How'd it go?" I asked her.

"The shooting was fine, but Pete's just barely holding it together."

"I'm not surprised."

"I got him to open up a bit. He just feels like he's let his family down."

"He hasn't done anything wrong." *As long as you don't count obstructing justice*, I thought.

"I think you need to go see him," Cara said.

I wanted to, but I just didn't know if it was a good idea. "Let me get through today and I'll think about it."

Edward Landon lived in an upscale neighborhood near the Leon County line that was home to a lot of professionals who worked in Tallahassee, but wanted to live in a rural setting with lower property taxes. That winter, one of the homes in the area had been the scene of a stomach-churning murder where the body had been found in a hot tub several days after death. Even now, I felt my guts roll over as we drove past it.

Landon's house was a tasteful brick Federal that had been built within the last ten years. The house was on the smaller end of the scale compared to other homes in the area, but the property was at least ten acres and nicely kept. The drive up to the house was lined with dogwoods that still showed a few white flowers among the fresh bright green foliage.

Darlene rang the bell and a man of average height wearing a polo shirt and slacks answered the door. "I'm Ed Landon. Come on in."

We followed him into the dining room where various boxes of papers and files were scattered about. A laptop was open on the table.

"Have a seat. You say you actually have two cases?" Landon was as unassuming in his mannerisms and speech as he was in his dress.

"Well… yes, but possibly only one killer," I said, and Darlene gave me a *what the hell* look. I realized that I probably should have at least given her the broad outline of what I was thinking before bringing it up with Landon. "I think there is at least a remote chance that they may be linked," I finished, sending Darlene a mental apology.

"I know I'm not privy to all the facts in the Baxter case, but I'm not sure I see how," Darlene said.

"Honestly, I'm not sure I do either. I hate the word, but I guess you could call it a hunch," I said.

"Fair enough," Landon said. "I'll keep that in mind when I'm reviewing them. But I think every case needs to be looked at individually, regardless. It doesn't matter if the same killer committed both crimes; they're still two separate murders. Same murderer, but different victims, different times, maybe different weapons and, in some cases, different motives."

I was taking a quick liking to Landon and his reasonable approach.

"First, tell me about the boy's murder."

Darlene and I gave him the rough timeline of events and covered the details we considered to be most relevant.

"Interesting. One question is, is there a connection between the events of that afternoon and the murder? No matter what people say, coincidences do occur. And if there is a connection, then what is it? It wouldn't have to mean that Pete Henley committed the murder. Perhaps one of the many people who saw the altercation was incensed by the boy's actions and decided to kill him for Jenny or for Deputy Henley."

"But you really don't see what Todd did in the videos."

"Okay, but if it's someone who knows and likes Pete, they would assume that Todd had to have done something horrible to evoke that kind of reaction out of him. Let's not get bogged down in the details right now. My point is just that, if there is a connection, it doesn't automatically mean that Pete is the murderer. Maybe someone who was there saw Harper touch the girl. Does she have any other admirers? Were they present?"

I had to admit that I hadn't thought of that. I could tell by Darlene's expression that she hadn't either.

"We think there's a good chance that the weapon was a baseball bat," Darlene said, and I thought of the item sitting in a safe deposit box with my name on it.

"Having the murder weapon would be a huge advantage," Landon said, and I felt as if he was talking directly to me. "If the killer used a baseball bat, that would certainly increase the chances that the two events were linked."

"We don't have the autopsy report yet, but, from the notes, can you make anything of the method of attack?"

"Impersonal. Purposeful. Quick. I don't think you can say whether the killer and the victim knew each other or not, but I wouldn't say the murderer hated him *or* loved him. There's no sign of overkill and the killer left the body out in the open and made no attempt to cover it up or move the remains. There's a possibility he might have been interrupted. Maybe the killer intended to mutilate the body, cover it up or move it, but he got spooked."

"He?"

"I would say he. A blunt object and a killing blow. Not definitive, but likely."

We talked a little more about the Harper murder before we reached a point where Landon said that he'd rather not speculate any more before he'd read through the notes that we'd brought with us.

Darlene agreed to wait outside while I went over the Baxter case with Landon. I just laid out the facts, not trying to push him one way or another.

"I see where you were coming from suggesting that the two cases could be linked. There are similarities between the two victims. Both are marginalized, both made enemies easily and almost relished fighting with others. For that matter, both were stingy with their money."

"The differences are obvious. One is young and one is old. Rich and poor. Male and female."

"Could it be a purposeful contrast? The killer was looking for two victims that were hateful in much the same way, but very much opposites physically. My main problem with your serial killer hypothesis is that these killings were passionless. A serial killer usually kills from the heart. He has a desire to kill."

He must have seen the look on my face. "I know how it sounds. But a serial killer does it for lust or the thrill. That's the motivation that can drive a murderer to pick victims that are unrelated to him or to each other. I'm ignoring the type of serial killer that does it for money. Those are usually caught pretty quickly because law enforcement is very good at following a money trail. Those killers usually only get a large body count if they move around and are able to avoid prosecution. Mind you, I said avoid prosecution, not detection. Very often they *are* detected. Like the husband who kills multiple wives for the insurance. He's always identified, but sometimes he's able to convince everyone that he's innocent. That is a very different kind of creature from the thrill killer. Those are the ones whose crimes allow him to go undetected in the same area for years."

I couldn't help thinking of Winston, the thrill killer who'd lived in our midst for decades. I shuddered at the memory and said, "I just want you to consider the single killer theory when you go through the two files."

Landon nodded, then said, "Just before I retired from teaching, I wrote several papers about the use of social media in murder cases. Both as a tool for law enforcement and as a tool for criminals to target victims. I think that was an important factor here. I know that the incident between Henley and Harper was spread through the Internet, but I also understand that there is a video that has been shared locally of Chief Maxwell and Mrs. Baxter arguing at a city commission meeting. Of course, these days we can assume that everything we do in public is being filmed, and it's becoming less surprising when a viral video is part of a murder case."

Darlene and I left Landon with his assurance that he'd have a preliminary analysis of the two cases by Monday. I dropped Darlene off at the office and decided to go by Pete's house. It wasn't the smartest thing I could do, but after what Cara had told me, I wanted to touch base with him. Even if all I did was give him a stupid pep talk, it might make him feel better.

I knocked on his door and Kim answered. When she saw me, she quickly stepped outside and closed the door.

"I've got some ideas about who the killer might be. I bet he was into drugs. Maybe Todd ripped off his dealer. Have you looked into that?" All of this poured out of her in breathless haste.

"We're looking into all of Todd's nefarious connections," I told her.

"You know Dad didn't kill him, right?"

"Yes, I know that your dad's innocent," I assured her.

"Some of the people on Twitter think he did it."

"People on Twitter don't solve murder cases for a living. Your dad and I do. And we're going to find—"

Before I could finish, the door opened again. "Larry," Pete said, sounding surprised. "Why are you keeping him out here? I hope you aren't trying to convince him to take you on as a partner," he said to Kim.

"No. But—"

"Go on inside."

"Don't worry," I told Kim and gave her a thumbs-up.

She nodded and went in the house.

"If I let her, she'd be driving all over town, rousting people out of their houses and asking them if they know who killed Todd Harper." There was more than a hint of pride in his voice.

"I know it must be hard on your family."

Pete grabbed my arm and walked me about twenty feet from the house. "Tell me we didn't majorly screw ourselves over the other morning," he said in a rough whisper.

"We're going to make this right. Somehow."

"We don't have a choice. I can't sleep. I've never been in a jam like this." I could hear the desperation in his voice.

"I'm not going to tell you too much, but we have reached out for some help on the case. Dad authorized us to bring in a consultant who's done profiling work for a lot of departments."

"A profiler?" he said suspiciously.

"I know some of them aren't worth any more than a psychic, but this guy's done some good work. I've met him and he's pretty grounded."

"Then good. The more help, the better, and the sooner this nightmare is over, the sooner things can go back to normal for my family. It's really been awful. Most people have been great, but there's a few that are real assholes. The girls haven't said much, but a couple of times I know they've seen some pretty hateful stuff on the Internet."

"With a little luck, the worst is over. We'll get on the trail of the real killer soon. We just need the lab reports and to dig deeper into Todd's life." I wasn't going to mention the private detective that the family had hired. Pete had enough to worry about.

I went in to say hi to Sarah and gave her a hug. I didn't see Jenny, but Sarah said she'd been spending almost all of her time in her bedroom. A teenager's bedroom can be a sanctuary from all the scary stuff that lives in the world outside. There's a lot to be said for having a good hiding place.

CHAPTER TWELVE

Friday morning started well. Dad texted me that he had sent out a press release announcing that the department had called in a consultant to help with the current murder cases. This was a good move—it made Dad appear proactive to the community and made it clear that the department was using all of the available resources that it could. On top of that, Shantel reported that they had identified a number of hairs from Todd's clothes that didn't appear to match any of his roommates' hair or Pete's.

Since Mrs. Baxter's house was so close to downtown, I'd checked with any businesses on the square and the nearby streets that might have had video cameras that could have captured someone coming or going from her house. I was driving around collecting the recordings when my phone rang and the caller ID told me that it was Steve Winter, the private detective. I was feeling upbeat and decided to talk to him.

"I've got some information that might be of interest to you," he said.

"If you have evidence in the case, then you need to turn it over to me."

"That's real funny coming from you."

His words caused a cold chill to run down my back. "Whatever you have to say, say it."

"I want to meet with you and I want you to tell me exactly what you're doing on this case. Because I have evidence that you and your old partner might be hiding something."

This presented me with a dilemma. Did I agree to meet with him, which would practically be an admission that he was right; or did I blow him off in an attempt at a bluff and risk not finding out what he had?

"Where?" I finally asked.

"Meet me at the Express Burgers. One hour," Winter said and hung up.

The number and variety of four-letter words that went through my mind would have impressed a particularly vulgar sailor. My first thought was to call Pete and warn him, but I quickly discarded that idea. I didn't know the extent of the threat and I didn't want to worry him if I didn't have to. Next I thought that I should just walk into Dad's office and lay it all out, but this didn't just involve me. I'd be putting Pete's life into the meat grinder too. The only thing to do now was to meet with Winter and find out just how deep a hole I was in.

I was in the parking lot of the Express Burgers fifteen minutes early. Winter showed up a few minutes later, parked next to me and got out. It wasn't hard to know it was him. He looked like someone had dialed up central casting and asked for an ex-Texas law man. He was even wearing the requisite jeans, cowboy hat and boots.

"I'm going to grab something for lunch. Do you want anything?" he asked. I thought it was an odd start to a blackmail meeting.

"No. I'm fine." Actually, I *was* pretty hungry, but the Express had the worst food in town. The place was always lucky to pass its health inspection, and usually only did on its third or fourth try, depending on how many rats were found the first couple of times. I thought about warning Winter, but wasn't feeling that charitable toward him at the moment.

I sat there and stewed, waiting for him to come back with his heart attack in a bag. At last he returned and sat down in my car.

"Hope you don't mind if I start eating," he said. I thought about the rats and told him to be my guest.

"I'd really like to get this over with. Or at least find out what this is about."

"Son, you got to understand that you've stepped in it. It's going to take you a while to get the stink off."

"What are we talking about?" I asked, already getting sick of his Texas Ranger folksiness.

He put down his food, picked up his phone and brought up a video. "Everything is a lot clearer on a full size monitor, but I think you'll get the idea. You having been there and all." He handed me the phone.

On the screen I could just make out a blurry figure walking from the back of a house. The figure was me and the house was Pete's. I was carrying a bag. The image was static and just showed a corner of Pete's house and part of the driveway.

"You all met, went around back and you came back a while later carrying an evidence bag. You can make all of that out pretty clearly when you view a larger image. Trust me."

"Where did you get this?" My heart was racing.

"Come on, you're a better investigator than that. One of Pete's neighbors has a security camera. It's across the street and one house over. But it picks up the corner of Pete's house and driveway."

"If you think you're going to blackmail me, you are seriously mistaken," I said, taking out my phone.

"Whoa! What'cha doing?"

"I'm calling my supervisor, Lt. Johnson, so that he can come over with some other deputies and arrest you for obstruction of justice."

"You understand what will happen if you do that?"

"I am well aware that I'll be charged with the same

violation."

"And your friend?"

I hesitated for a moment. "Pete would tell me to call."

"Good to hear. Put down that phone for a couple of minutes and let me explain a few other things."

Reluctantly, I put the phone down. "I'm listening."

"The neighbor's video was also running the night of Todd's murder. What it doesn't show is your friend going anywhere that night. Now, he could have gone out through his backyard to the other street, gotten a car somehow and driven over there to whomp that boy over the head. But I doubt it. That's one thing. The other piece of the puzzle that gives me pause is the fact that you bagged up whatever evidence you found at the house. I can't make it out in the video, but it seems pretty clear that you're saving it. And I don't think you're going to use it to blackmail your friend."

"We should have canvassed Pete's neighborhood after the murder," I said, feeling like a dumbass.

"Yep. If you had, you would have learned about the camera. So I asked myself, why did you bag up some evidence at your friend's house? If you all knew he was guilty and were going to cover it up, you would have just destroyed whatever you found. I think you know he's innocent and are crossing a line to help him."

I started to defend my actions, but he held up a hand to stop me.

"I've had a couple of partners over the years that I would probably do the same thing for. Maybe not in such a stupid way. But still… I get it."

"So what's the point? Why are we sitting here?"

"I've been hired to find this boy's killer. I'm going to do my job and I think you might be able to help me."

"I'm not going to break the law to help you earn your pay."

"But you're willing to break the law to help your friend. We've established that. This is a two birds with one stone opportunity for you."

"What are we talking about? What do you want from me?" I still felt like he had his foot on my neck, but clearly his motives were a bit more pure than I had originally believed.

"All I want is information… Now don't go getting all riled up. I was an investigator for a lot of years and I don't expect you to give me a bunch of the details. Just the broad strokes, and not just about this murder. I also need information on the old woman who was killed." He delivered the last line casually, as though it didn't change the complexity of the situation.

"Wait a minute. Why do you want information about the Baxter murder?"

"I got you by the short hairs, son. The information highway ain't always going to be a two-way road. I'm trusting that you and your buddy aren't involved in a murder conspiracy, even though I got a certain amount of proof to that effect. I'm asking you to trust me on this. I need that information. May be nothing. But if I determine it's important, I'll explain my reasoning."

I looked him in the eye and tried to assess his honesty, though I knew better. There are people in the world who can lie and seem more sincere and honest than someone else who's telling the truth. But that didn't stop me from trying.

"Do you think the murders are connected?"

"Honestly, I don't know."

"But you suspect it?"

"That doesn't take a Sherlock Holmes level of detecting."

"What do you want to know?"

"Give me the lay of the land first. I may have some questions when you get done."

I did as he asked, giving him the general layout of the crime scenes, the victims and the damage done to the bodies. I didn't tell him much more than I would have a reporter.

"Would you say that these killings were done out of passion?"

"No. That was one of the similarities I noticed."

"Quick?"

"Almost assuredly."

"Is there someone that looks guilty for the second murder?"

"Yes."

"Okay, thanks." He looked down at what remained of his lunch. "This is cow crap," he said, putting it back in the bag and crumpling it up.

"The Deep Pit Bar-b-que or the Donut Hole are the best bets around here. The new taco stand isn't too bad either. Sorry, I could have warned you about this place."

He got out of the car. "Not a problem. I'll be in touch." He headed for the nearest trashcan.

Now what? I thought.

My phone buzzed with a text: *Getting ready to leave. Come over and you can get Mauser.* I texted back to Dad that I'd be there in an hour.

I returned to the office and tried to concentrate on the Baxter murder. I followed up on Madge's sister's alibi, making sure that she was really in Savannah that morning. She certainly had the hate in her heart to have done the deed, but with Savannah being a good five hours away, it wasn't hard to get a witness or two that placed her far enough away to eliminate her.

I requested a warrant for Madge Baxter's financial records and made up a list of people I wanted to question about Madge, including the three organizations that she'd left money to.

I got to Dad's house a little later than I had planned.

"I packed all of his stuff in the van," Dad said as I followed him back into the house.

"Hey, Larry," Genie greeted me. She was brushing Mauser and telling him to be a good boy. I had to bite my tongue not to say anything. I could tell that having Genie around was not going to make Mauser any less spoiled. Mauser looked at me as though to say, *See, you better treat me right or I'll tell my friends.*

"Okay, Mr. Prima Donna, are you ready to go?"

He trotted over to me.

"We'll follow you over to your place so you can have both your car and the van if you need to take Mauser someplace," Dad said. "Then we've got to stop in Tallahassee and check in on Genie's son before we hit the road."

Genie had lived with her husband and her son a few doors down from us when I was young. Her son had Down Syndrome and Genie had brought him with her when she came to babysit me.

"Where is Jimmy living now?" I asked Genie as Mauser bumped into me excitedly.

"He shares a house with a couple of other guys. He's doing really well," she said proudly.

"I'd like to go by and see him sometime."

"He'd love that. When your father met him again, he remembered you. He works at the library on the east side of town."

Dad walked by us, carrying a small gym bag and a slightly larger suitcase. We all followed him out of the house. "How are things going?" he asked, and I knew he was asking about the cases.

"Good," I said, not wanting to even hint at the odd direction things had taken. Let him enjoy his weekend. Despite my best effort, something in my tone must have alerted him. He gave me a sideways look that plainly said he wanted to ask more, but was going to let it go for now.

When we got to my place, Dad got out of the van, said goodbye to Mauser and left the dog inside. "Don't let him out until we're out of sight," he told me, getting into Genie's car.

Did he think that Mauser was going to run after the car like an overgrown Lassie? But I didn't say a word, letting the man have his delusions.

I waited as requested, then let Mauser out to do his

business while I hauled his food and bag of toys into the house. I swear Dad had bought every toy that the Kong company ever made. Of course, since Mauser had the potential to chew his house down to toothpicks, I understood.

"Come on, you big lug. The rest of your fan club will be here later, but for now you're stuck with me and Ivy," I told him while he sniffed around the old live oaks that surrounded the rise where my trailer sat. It was a beautiful afternoon and I allowed myself to dream of someday building a house under those oaks. Did I see Cara with me on the porch of that house? Of course, right now the betting odds were that I'd be fired and possibly jailed before that could ever happen. No house and no conjugal visits with Cara at Raiford.

"Okay, big guy, let's go in. I want to get some work done this afternoon." I still had almost two hours before Cara and Alvin would arrive.

I sat on the couch with my laptop while Ivy lay beside me. Mauser, denied the opportunity to get up on the couch by Ivy's iron glare, sat in front of me and stared.

"I'm not going to move her. If you want to sit on the couch, you'll have to convince her to move. Don't stare at me," I told him.

I did a background check on our Texas Ranger. His record was stellar, with several commendations both for heroic acts and successful investigations. For most of his career, he appeared to have worked in armed robbery and violent crimes. He'd retired a few years ago. I looked hard at the picture that came up. It was several years old now, but I was sure it was the same man. I did a Google search, but couldn't come up with a website for any detective agency connected with his name. *How did the Bells find him?* I wondered.

"Okay, fine." Mauser had upped his game, moving closer to me and attempting to drool on my laptop. "Ivy, why don't you get on the back of the couch?" I nudged her. She looked at me like I was a traitor, but got up and tried to walk across my keyboard. "Now don't you start."

She finally settled on the arm of the couch and Mauser clamored his way up beside me, using his big butt to push me to the very end.

"Everybody happy now?"

Neither of them even looked at me.

I dug out my phone and called Mrs. Bell. She demanded to know if we'd made any progress.

"We're doing everything we can right now. Lab reports take time."

"Has Mr. Winter talked to you?" she asked, sounding like she expected an argument.

"He has. That's why I'm calling. I'm curious how you came to hire him."

"If you think we're going to sit back and wait while you all dither around, not finding the man who killed my boy… especially when it might be someone that's working for you…"

"No, no, I'm not upset that you hired him. I'm just gathering some information and was interested in how you decided to hire this particular private detective."

"Well, I don't… Mother told me about him. I think a friend or… I'll ask her." She started talking to her mother, loud enough that I could hear them over the phone.

"Mother, where did you find Mr. Winter?"

"Who wants to know?"

"It's that deputy with the sheriff's office."

"What business is it of his?"

"Mother, he just wants to know."

"He called me," she said.

"He called you? When?"

"While you were at the funeral home."

"I thought he was recommended by Paul."

"I never got the chance to call the man that Paul suggested. Mr. Winter called me up, told me who he was and offered to help. His prices were very reasonable. What are you looking at me like that for?"

The younger Mrs. Bell came back on the phone. "Mother says—"

"I heard her."

"You're looking into his background?" She sounded a bit worried. "He's not a conman or anything, is he?"

"No. I really am just doing some routine checking. He seems to be just as advertised."

"Oh, okay. Please let us know as soon as there's any news," she said, and I assured her that I would.

"Curiouser and curiouser, gang," I said to my two companions, who were both sound asleep.

My phone rang. I didn't recognize the number, but it was local.

"Deputy Macklin?" I heard a familiar voice, but I wasn't sure who it was. "It's Chief Maxwell." That explained it. I'd heard him a hundred times, but never over the phone.

"I understand that you can't give me any details about the investigation. However, I was hoping that, as a professional courtesy, you could give me a general idea of how it's going."

His request sounded rehearsed. It was very strange to sense insecurity from a man whose ego was rivaled only by those of the rulers of ancient Rome.

"Chief, I'm sure that there are many things about this investigation that have you worried. Like how long will your neighbor's house be draped in crime scene tape? Will we solve it before the election in the fall? Or will we discover that you killed her?" I said drolly, unable to resist baiting him.

"Listen, you assho… Look, I just wanted to make sure that you didn't need anything else from me. I know that you and your dad are professionals and won't use this as a political opportunity. I truly appreciate that."

I bet you do, since I wouldn't be quite so confident that you wouldn't use it if the roles were reversed, I thought. Aloud, I said, "I'll want to have a formal interview with you. Monday. Tuesday at the latest."

I could almost hear the calculations running in his head. I decided to give him a small break. "Pick a time and we can do it on the quiet. We won't make a big deal about you coming in to be questioned as a witness in a murder. All on the down-low."

"Okay. Monday, first thing. Nine o'clock."

"That works for me."

He hung up and I heard a car coming up the drive. Mauser, the masterful guard dog that he was, lifted his head up off the couch long enough to ascertain that it was an automobile, gave a little huff that was more *Go away, don't bother me* than *Get off my property* and promptly went back to sleep.

But the giant's sleep was thoroughly interrupted when Alvin came charging in, excited at the sight of Mauser. They sniffed each other, then Alvin jumped up on top of Mauser, who looked a little panicked. I couldn't help but laugh.

CHAPTER THIRTEEN

Due to a scheduling fluke at the vet's, Cara had a rare second Saturday in a row off from work. We debated over breakfast how to spend the day and decided on a trip to Tallahassee with the dogs. I had some work on the Baxter case planned for Sunday, but today I wanted to enjoy a little downtime with Cara.

We all piled into the van and headed for Lake Ella, a park located in the city's midtown area next to the Tallahassee Police Department. The sidewalk that curved around the small lake was a favorite walking spot for humans and canines.

The beautiful weather continued, with a clear sky and gentle breeze. The park was crowded with families, walkers and joggers. Walking Mauser in public was like holding up a sign that read "free money." People gathered around us as we walked and, over and over again, we stopped to repeat his stats, including his weight, how much he ate and that, yes, Great Danes came in black and white. We also had to tell a few well-meaning kids that, no, they couldn't ride him. It was overwhelming, but also quite a bit of fun to talk to people who normally would have walked right on by. Many of them had their own Great Dane story or two. Luckily for

Alvin, he was cute enough and forward enough that he managed to get a share of the laughs and attention showered on the elephant dog.

After two trips around the lake, with Mauser now so tired that he walked as far behind us as his leash would permit, we did a little window shopping at the cottage shops on the edge of the lake, then decided to indulge in some ice cream from Barb's Gourmet Brittles. Alvin and Mauser had to get by with dog treats.

Sitting at a picnic table, I looked over at Cara, admiring her smiling eyes and her hair glowing in the sun.

"I'll tell you what's bothering me about us moving in together right now," I said, deciding to tackle the issue at the risk of spoiling a beautiful day.

"What's that?" she asked, not sounding too defensive. Her eyes concentrated on the ice cream cone.

"I don't want us to do this just because your lease is up. If we're going to take that big of a step in our relationship, I want to do it because it's what we both desire." I paused and she looked up at me. "Does that make sense?"

"I guess. Though I wasn't suggesting it just to keep from paying rent." She looked a little hurt that I would even think that.

"I know you weren't. But it just felt like you were pushing it based on your lease and not necessarily because of your feelings. I know it's supposed to be the woman in the relationship that's hung up about feelings, but I've made mistakes in the past by letting a relationship get pushed by outside forces."

"I get what you're saying. But I *do* have to make a decision soon, and if I sign the lease then it would be like saying we aren't going to do anything for at least a year. Right now it may seem like I'm pushing a little, but a year is a long time."

I wanted to say that leases could be broken, but that wasn't a good attitude. Was she pushing the relationship? Or was I just dragging my feet?

"I've got a lot on my plate right now," I said, and it sounded lame even to my ears. True, but lame.

"I know that. But when won't you?" she asked, and I knew that we were getting dangerously close to the issue we'd had over my job when we'd first met.

"You're right. I don't know what to say. I just… feel that something isn't right about making the decision now."

"I guess I'll sign the lease then," Cara said after a while. There was a sadness in her voice that hurt all the more since I knew that my hesitation was causing it.

"Don't do it yet. You still have a couple of weeks," I said, trying to smooth things over and regretting that I'd brought up the topic.

"But if you've made your decision…" she said, hitting me over the head with logic.

"I don't know," I said pathetically.

"I'm not mad," she said, sounding melancholy, which was much worse than if she'd been mad.

I put my hand on her knee. "I love you. And I'm sorry I'm an idiot," I said and got a small smile in return.

"I love you too," she said and leaned in for a kiss. "And I'm *really* sorry that you're an idiot," she teased.

Mauser had had enough of the human prattle and decided to get up and turn in circles, tangling himself up in poor Alvin's leash. We got up and separated the leashes before Alvin was choked or crushed.

During the ride home we listened to our favorite classic rock station while the dogs snored in the back of the van, managing to recapture some of the golden glow of spending a spring day with the one you love.

On Sunday I texted Pete and we arranged to meet at the Donut Hole. I'd decided that, considering what we'd already done, I didn't care anymore about whether it was right to talk with him about the case. Plus, I wanted to fill him in on the crazy assist we were getting from the ex-Texas Ranger.

Pete looked a little more like his old self. Of course, that might have been due to the fact that he was eating a freshly baked glazed masterpiece. I ordered half a dozen and a cup of coffee, then sat across from Pete at a picnic table underneath a sprawling pecan tree, well away from any other customers. For a moment I just enjoyed my coffee and Bavarian crème.

"Okay. That's better," I said, setting the coffee and what was left of the donut down on the table.

"You eating all of those?"

"Half are for Cara. She's at home babysitting the animals. We have Mauser this weekend."

"How are things going with her? You know, if you screw up this relationship, I'm going to consider you a world-class dumbass."

"We're doing pretty well. Thanks for asking," I said with a smile.

"So…?"

I told Pete all about the meeting with Winter, trying to downplay the period of time when I thought we were going to be blackmailed.

"And you didn't let me back you up when you were meeting with a potential blackmailer?" I guess it hadn't been hard for him to read between the lines.

"You were already pretty stressed out. I didn't think you needed to know that someone was about to blow our lives completely out of the water."

"We did it to ourselves. I should have just let you take the evidence and log it in."

"Too late to worry about that. I really think that this Winter guy is all right."

"I should have thought about that surveillance camera. I noticed it a while back when I was putting out the garbage, but I didn't know that it caught the corner of our house. Branson is a jerk. He's the most obnoxious guy in the neighborhood."

"But he had some evidence that, while it doesn't clear you completely, makes it a lot less likely that you snuck off and killed Harper," I said and then added, "Not that I needed any evidence."

"Shut up." He threw a napkin at me. "Why do you think Winter contacted the Bells?"

"I don't know, but I'm going to ask him the next time I see him."

"How's it feel to have Maxwell in the hot seat?"

"Kind of nice. I'd be enjoying it a lot more if it wasn't for all the politics of the upcoming election. I could tighten the thumbscrews down another twist or two. But also, with you in about the same predicament, I can kind of empathize with the big jerk."

"There are definitely some similarities between our situations," Pete mused.

"Similarities, but I can't find any connections. That's what I'm going to spend the rest of today looking into."

"Small county, there's bound to be places where the two victims' lives intersected."

"If they were two normal folks in the county, that would be true. But here we've got a guy who wasn't really a member of the community. At least not long term. And then we have Baxter, who had been in the community for forever, but she was old and cantankerous. And she was so mean that she didn't have any more friends than Harper did."

"You're right No one liked her. I hate to pull Maxwell out of the fire, but, really, she had more enemies than Stalin and for pretty much the same reasons."

"Back to Harper. Where did Jenny meet him? Certainly not at school."

"A friend of hers, Cheyanne, graduated last year and is going to Tallahassee Community College. Jenny met Todd at Cheyanne's birthday party about four months ago. They started texting and all that crap. When they started dating, Jenny led me to believe that he was a classmate. Trust me, when I found out the truth, she and I had a long talk about misleading your parents. Told her I'd rather we had a fight than for her to be sneaking around. Anyway, by the time that

I learned that Todd was trouble, Jenny was already trying to put some distance between them."

"He didn't have a regular job. I wonder if he ever did any part-time or day labor with a yard or construction crew, something that would have brought him into contact with Madge."

"Time to go back to the roommates?"

"Dereck had the closest relationship with him. Also, maybe Hex would know, though I get the feeling she didn't socialize with him much."

"Maybe they talked about his life when they were traveling to her clients."

"Worth checking. I'd like to talk with Jenny too."

"I was afraid you'd say that. Tell you what, I'll try to get her to the office today. Probably be better if you talked to her somewhere less emotionally volatile than the house."

"She won't give you a hard time about coming in to talk to me?"

"Right now, Jenny's vacillating between blaming me for a lot of this and blaming herself. I've been willing to let her put the guilt on me. Hell, I put a lot of it on myself. I'd rather have her mad at me than angry at herself to the point that she spirals down into depression. But I can push the guilt button enough to get her to come in. Will two o'clock work?"

I agreed, then returned home bearing the donuts. I met a robed and sleepy-headed Cara watching the dogs sniff and play in the yard.

"Donuts! You're my hero," she said, giving me a kiss.

"What about all that hippy health food your mother pushes? Are you sure you should have all this sugar?" I teased, holding the bag away from her.

"The blood of my Viking ancestors demands sugar and carbs and lots of them. Gimme," she said, snatching at the bag.

"Careful, that robe is going to come open."

"I'm wearing jammies, you pervert," she laughed.

I sighed and gave her the bag of donuts, then headed back out to meet Darlene at the office.

I talked with Darlene about trying to find a connection between the two victims and she agreed that it was worth a shot. While I was not officially assigned to Todd's case anymore, since I was technically working my case, we agreed it was okay to skirt the rules. She got Dereck on the first try and he agreed to meet us at his house.

"Do you know if Todd ever did any day labor or worked for a landscaping business, maybe a plumber or something like that?" I asked him.

Dereck gave us a little smile. "I don't want to say anything bad about the guy, with him being dead and all, but work wasn't his thing. I never saw him even try to do manual labor, of any kind. Really, you all are on the wrong track there."

"Did you ever hear him mention a woman named Madge Baxter?"

"No. He was always being a dog about girls. Talking up this one or that one. I didn't always listen, but that's kind of an odd name. I think I would have remembered it."

"She wasn't that kind of girl. She was an old woman."

"No, man, he didn't go for the cougars."

"This would not have been a sex thing. She was an old woman who lived downtown. Anything about that ring a bell?"

"Sorry, no. He was so self-involved. Unless there was sex or the possibility of easy money, he wasn't interested."

Easy money. Mrs. Baxter had money. Could that have been the connection? Had Todd thought he had a way of getting at her cash? Seemed like a thin possibility.

"Did he seem to have any extra cash lately? Or did he mention that he'd be getting his hands on some money?"

"Todd was always coming into money. A money cow was just around the next corner. People believed him the first dozen times he said it. But, no, he didn't have anything that seemed real. Besides, when he said he had a scheme, it usually involved running girls or drugs. But he didn't have any big contacts and he was too lazy to go get them. There *was* the one girl. Do you know about that? 'Cause I don't want to get her in trouble."

"Hex," Darlene said and Dereck nodded.

We left no wiser than when we had arrived.

On the way back to the office, I gave Darlene the low-down on Winter, minus the hiding evidence part. Hopefully that would never need to see the light of day.

"You should have talked to me first. I didn't think much of that guy when I talked to him. Do I have to remind you that I'm the lead investigator on this case?" Darlene was annoyed and she had every right to be. But I didn't want to be running around behind her back any more than I already had. "Why did he want to talk to you so badly?"

"I don't know. Probably because my dad's the sheriff. He might have felt I had an inside track." The dad excuse could come in handy sometimes.

"I want to meet him."

"If it's okay with you, I'd like to be there when you do and ask him why he wanted to get involved in this case. I don't think it's just for the money."

"Why don't you arrange something for Monday?" she suggested.

"Okay. And Pete's bringing Jenny to the office at two o'clock today," I told her.

"You sure have been busy on my case. Hate to tell you, but I haven't been working on yours at all." She still sounded miffed.

"I'm not trying to meddle," I protested. "I've just got this bug in my head that the two cases are connected."

"Okay, it wasn't like I had any plans for my Sunday afternoon."

CHAPTER FOURTEEN

We were waiting in the conference room when Pete and Jenny arrived. It was a bit awkward, with Pete being both a suspect and the father of a juvenile witness. He had every right to insist on being present while we interviewed his daughter, but as investigators, we didn't want to interview a witness in front of a suspect. But Pete trusted us and Jenny agreed to being questioned without her father present.

"We appreciate you coming in," Darlene started off. "I know how difficult this must be for you. The death of someone you knew, the embarrassing video showing your dad not at his best, and then the stigma of having him as a suspect in the murder."

"No kidding." Jenny gave us a sad smile.

"Where and when did you meet Todd?"

She repeated the same basic facts that Pete had given to me.

"Does the name Madge Baxter sound familiar?"

"I've heard of her. And I know she was killed soon after Todd."

"What had you heard about her prior to her murder?"

"I had a friend in middle school, Sherry Kirby, whose father worked for Mrs. Baxter. Her dad took her over there a couple of times to help him. He paints houses. Sherry said that Mrs. Baxter was a witch. Remember, this was back in sixth grade, and she managed to convince a lot of the kids that it was true. She said that Mrs. Baxter cheated her father too."

"Anything else?" Darlene asked, and Jenny looked down at the table. "Anything at all would help."

"Not really. It's silly, but if I tell you something, I'd rather you didn't tell my dad."

"Mum's the word," I said.

"One Halloween, right after Sherry had really started telling everyone that Mrs. Baxter was a witch, I was staying over at Sherry's house. We were going to go trick-or-treating with a couple other girls. When we went out, Sherry convinced us to go egg Mrs. Baxter's house. Sherry had about three dozen eggs. I think her dad had given them to her. I figured out that he wanted us to ruin the paint job he'd done on her house."

"Okay. Anything else?" I asked.

She pursed her lips and seemed to concentrate for a few seconds, then her eyes opened wide. "You know, I think I *did* hear someone talking about her once when I was with Todd. I didn't think about it right away because they were calling her Mrs. Bastard."

I think my ears literally perked up. "Who was talking about her?" I asked, trying not to sound too eager.

"Geez, I don't know. I was kind of… tired and not really listening 'cause it didn't have anything to do with me." Jenny paused. "That sounds awful. But you know what I mean."

I assured her that I did.

"Who was with you?" Darlene asked.

"The usual. His roommates, maybe a couple of others. Probably Anna." Jenny's brow furrowed as she tried to remember the conversation.

"I think it was one of the roommates. Dereck or David. It was kind of early on, so on top of everything else, I wasn't real sure who was who at that point. But they were, like, really bitching about her. I think whichever one it was was supposed to get paid. Hey, that probably means it was a Friday, which makes sense we'd be partying." She looked guilty. "Not that I party that much."

I was glad that Pete hadn't hung around. This was hard enough for Jenny to talk about.

"Anything else? Did they ever talk about her again?"

"No. At least, not around me."

We went down a dozen more avenues that all turned out to be dead ends, then reunited Jenny with her father and said our goodbyes. Then I turned to Darlene.

"So do you think that Dereck was lying to us?" I asked.

"If so, he was pretty damn cool about it," Darlene grumbled. She really hated people who lied to her face.

"If Jenny's right, then I don't see how he wouldn't have remembered Baxter's name."

"I think we need to have another little conversation with him," she said with a grim expression on her face.

I got on the phone and told Dereck that we needed to see him again. He complained about having a gaming session that afternoon, but I impressed upon him the necessity of us getting together and he finally agreed to meet at four.

While Darlene and I made a sad lunch of potato chips from the vending machine and a couple of apples, Edward Landon called and said that he had his preliminary reports done. Darlene told him that we were at the office if he wanted to come over now.

Landon arrived in less than thirty minutes. He had put together a brief on both murders. We sat down in the small conference room to talk.

"I wasn't sure that you all would want to meet on Sunday afternoon, but I figured this way you would have a head start on the week."

"Appreciate it," I said, just as my phone started to buzz. I picked it up off of the table and saw that the caller ID said it was Steve Winter. I had called him earlier and left a message for him that we wanted to meet on Monday. I excused myself and left the room to speak with him. He agreed to come in Monday morning.

Landon looked up when I came in and started right into his pitch.

"I wanted to talk to both of you together to begin with, so that way I can do my little introduction just one time." We nodded and he went on. "This is all very preliminary. It can't be anything else without all the lab reports. However, I compared what was in the witness statements, responding officer reports and your brief summaries and came up with some probabilities. I disagree with doing profiles that try to come to conclusions. I like to simply give the investigators percentages. What I do is take the data I'm given, compare it to past cases, and then provide you with probability estimates.

"So, for instance, on both of your cases I give a probability of gender. For the Harper case it's seventy-two percent male. That's based on the estimated strength of the blows to the head and a comparison of the average number of times that females or males have used baseball bats to commit murder." He paused to see if we were following him.

"I also took a few other things into account, such as height and age of the victim. For the Baxter case, I've made the probability of a male having committed the crime at ninety-one percent. This was a little trickier than the Harper case because there is less data on gardening shears being used as murder weapons and, while it took some strength to plunge the shears through her back, the victim was older and frail. That should give you a rough idea of how I work. Any questions?"

We shook our heads.

"Let's do Harper first," Darlene said.

We followed along in our copies of the report as Landon went over it. The bottom line was that the murderer was most likely a male between the ages of eighteen and fifty who held a grudge against the victim. The killer had no discernable mental illness or conditions beyond what would be considered average for the population. He'd probably made the decision to attack the victim during the prior twelve hours. He was average to tall in height and probably participated in some sort of regular outdoor activity. Landon reviewed a dozen more items, but they all fell within the average range.

"I'm sorry that there isn't anything extraordinary about your perp. Of course, I'll make adjustments after seeing the final autopsy and lab reports."

The report on Baxter wasn't much more enlightening. The only major adjustments were that it was almost certainly a male and that the age range narrowed to between twenty-five and forty-five.

"You might find this of interest. I created a graph of the overlay of the characteristics. Nothing in it would suggest that the murderer couldn't be the same person."

After he left, I looked at Darlene. "What do you think? Are we wasting the county's money?"

"I don't know. I admit I can't see how he helped us. Most of what he said was common sense."

We drove back to Dereck's place. David and Anna weren't anywhere around.

"David and Anna have been staying at her place. She says it creeps her out when she's here." Dereck sounded downcast.

"We've come across some more information," Darlene started. "I'm going to ask you a question, and you need to think very carefully before you answer." He nodded. "Since we're recording this, I need you to say your answers out loud."

I could tell that he was picking up on the fact that we weren't being quite as friendly as we'd been that morning.

"Yes. Sure, I'll think about your question," he said, sounding a little puzzled.

"First, I want you to know that we have talked with a witness who says that you were having a conversation about

Madge Baxter where everyone was referring to her as Mrs. Bastard. Does this ring any bells?"

He looked guilty as sin. "Yeah."

"Why did you pretend you didn't recognize the name when we questioned you earlier?" Darlene asked.

From the look in Dereck's eyes, I thought he was going to shut down and ask for a lawyer. "You're only interested in the murders, right?"

"Yes," Darlene and I said together. "Now tell us what your relationship with her was, and why you tried to hide it," I continued.

"Relationship? She, like, stole fifteen hundred dollars from me. I did a whole week's work for her, bought supplies and everything. I… yeah, I was pretty damn mad at her."

"When was this?"

"Three months ago. Something like that. I've tried to forget it."

"You didn't get your money back?"

"How? I don't have the time or money to go through all that small claims crap. Besides, when I started asking around, everyone told me to just let it go. She has a lawyer and will fight you tooth and nail. So what's the small guy going to do?"

"What did she owe you for?" Darlene asked.

"I repaired some flooring and siding on her house. Mostly just where dry rot had gotten into the wood. There was actually a bunch more work I was going to do for her, but luckily I'd said upfront that I needed to be paid by the week. I do a little carpentry when I can to pay for school, but I don't have money to carry over while I'm doing a big job. When she wouldn't pay for the first week, of course I quit. Guys at the hardware store got a good laugh. They said every new guy gets suckered into doing work for her. They swore that if I'd told them who I was working for, they would have warned me. I'm not so sure. They said it was a right of passage or some bullshit."

"And that's the end of it?"

"It pissed me off every time I thought about it for a month." He hesitated.

"What are you hiding?" Darlene asked. She did a very good impression of an angry mom. I was pretty sure that she was still pissed off at him for lying to us earlier.

"I broke into her shed and stole some stuff. It was stupid, and what I got was mostly junk anyway. But it made me feel better."

"When was this?"

"About a month ago?"

"Was Todd involved in the situation with Mrs. Baxter?"

"No. He listened to me gripe about it. That's all. I went on a couple of benders, wallowing in self pity about it, and he went with me, but he didn't have anything to do with stealing the stuff."

Something about the way Dereck said it made me wonder if maybe someone else did. "Was anyone else involved in the burglary?" I asked, watching him wince at the word burglary.

"I won't talk about it. Todd definitely wasn't and, as far as I know, he didn't know about it. Honestly, I wouldn't want Todd involved in something I wanted to keep on the down-low. He talked a lot when he was buzzed." Dereck's words had the ring of truth.

"No other connection?"

"No."

He gave us the names of a few other people who might have heard him talking about Mrs. Baxter, then Darlene and I called it a day.

The house was quiet when I got home. Cara had sent Mauser home with Dad and decided to spend the night at her place, so I spent the evening with Ivy reading *The Phantom Killer*, the true story of the 1950s murders in Texarkana that had inspired the movie *The Town That Dreaded Sundown*. A lot of things had changed in law enforcement since then, especially regarding the methods and resources available to investigate crimes. But then, as now, it often came down to simply luck, guts and determination. They never caught their killer. I hoped we'd have more luck.

On Monday, I arrived at the office both looking forward to and dreading the confrontation with Maxwell. I was going to enjoy grilling him, but I didn't look forward to having to step around all of the political pitfalls. And I was going to be on my own for this one. I would have liked to have Darlene sit in on it, but that wasn't possible so I asked Lt. Johnson if he'd mind being there as a witness in case Maxwell cried foul about anything later. Even with the interview being recorded, it would be nice to have another person in the room to keep things on the straight and narrow if I started to stray.

Johnson came over to my desk at ten minutes to nine. He stood ramrod straight in a perfectly clean and pressed uniform. Clearly his twenty years in the military hadn't been wasted.

"Ready," he said, more an order than a question.

"Yep," I said, purposely avoiding the more appropriate "yes, sir." I stood up and grabbed my notes.

"I'll let you ask the questions," Johnson said, which was good since I was planning on it.

We stood at the conference room door waiting on Maxwell. I'd debated using one of the interview rooms, but I reminded myself that I was going to play nice. We saw Maxwell push open the door at the end of the hall and stride down to us with an odd smirk on his face.

"Gentlemen," he greeted us.

"Maxwell," Johnson said.

Before I could say anything, Maxwell continued, "Before we get started, I think I should tell you that there is a dead body in your parking lot."

CHAPTER FIFTEEN

I wasn't sure that I'd understood him correctly. Had he gone crazy? Johnson gave me a look that told me I was to blame for whatever was going on.

"What?" I asked.

"I walked over here from my office and came through your parking lot. There's a car parked near the dumpster in the back corner. I noticed that there was someone slumped over in the seat. When I looked through the windshield, being careful not to touch the glass, I saw that the person was dead. Of course, I'm not a doctor, but he has a knife sticking in his chest, the wound is no longer bleeding and his eyes are open and glazed over."

I took a second to process his speech. "Son of a bitch!" I yelled and started for the door.

Ten minutes later there was a crowd surrounding the car. Dad stood back, fuming, while Shantel and Marcus took pictures. Several deputies kept their distance, looking grim. Nobody was making the usual morbid jokes. Having a person murdered in our parking lot wasn't funny, and it wouldn't instill confidence in the sheriff's office.

"Where the hell is Parks?" Dad demanded, looking like he wanted to strangle someone. "You say you know who the victim is?" he asked me.

"His name is Steve Winter. He's a retired Texas Ranger. And from what I could tell from looking through the window, he was stabbed through the heart. The knife is still lodged in his chest. Dr. Darzi is on his way."

"Any chance it was suicide?" he asked wistfully.

"On a scale of one to ten, with ten being most likely, I'd say it's a solid one and a half that it's suicide."

Major Sam Parks walked up and Dad turned to confront him.

"Sorry, I was on a conference call," Parks said. He was the senior administrator in the department and was acting sheriff when Dad wasn't available. He handled most of the managerial details involved with running the department.

"I want all of the security footage pulled, copied and reviewed," Dad said.

"This corner isn't covered," Parks answered, looking back at the building.

"What? You're telling me that there isn't one hundred percent coverage for the outside of our building?" Dad was livid and I felt some sympathy for Parks. One of his responsibilities was overseeing the buildings and grounds, including security.

"All points of entry and exit into the building are covered, including all the windows. Honestly, to get this corner, considering the trees and the dumpster, that would have required putting up another pole and camera. And after you add running the powerlines and the wiring, we'd be talking about five thousand dollars," Parks said reasonably.

Dad didn't like being reasoned with when he was in this foul of a mood. He was visibly grinding his teeth and staring daggers at Parks.

"Damn it all! All right, pull all body cam and car cam footage for anyone who went through this lot last night or this morning," he barked at Parks, who turned without a word and headed back inside to get it done. Like me, Parks had been around Dad long enough to know that he'd cool down eventually.

"You know the victim. Does that mean he's related to one of the cases you're working?" Dad asked me as we watched Shantel and Marcus dust the outside of the car for prints.

"He was working as a private detective for the Bells, Todd Harper's mother and grandmother. There were elements to his story that didn't quite fit. For instance, he contacted the Bells instead of them contacting him. I had only recently discovered this and was planning on asking him about it the next time I saw him."

"Did you do a background on him?" Dad asked and I wanted to tell him that I wasn't a moron. But now was not the time to give him a hard time.

"Yes. He checked out. Thirty years as a Texas Ranger. Distinguished career. However, I didn't find any signs that he was actively seeking employment as a private detective."

"So you think he had a personal interest in the Harper case?" Some of his anger was dissipating and being replaced by curiosity.

"Something drew him to the investigation," I said, wondering what we were going to find in his car. Was the video of me carrying the evidence bag still on his phone? His laptop?

Dr. Darzi arrived with two assistants. "Very smart. Have them get murdered in your own parking lot. Saves on time and gas," he said, but then saw the sour looks on our faces. "Not so funny when it happens in your own backyard, I guess." He shook his head. "Can we get to the car?" he asked Shantel.

"We're about done. Give us two seconds."

"Do you know how long the car has been here?" Darzi asked while we waited.

"We'll have an idea when we review the CCTV." While we didn't have any coverage where the car currently sat, we would be able to see when it drove into the lot.

Shantel started to open the car door.

"Wait," Darzi said. "Here, put this beside the body." He handed a thermometer to Shantel. The temperature inside the closed car could have been important when determining the time of death.

She opened the driver's door and, after setting the thermometer down, began dusting around the body as best she could. She needed to get whatever she could out of the car before Darzi and his team started moving the body.

Once Shantel gave the all-clear, they moved in, examined the body as best they could inside the car, then removed it carefully, trying to preserve any trace evidence.

"Dead at least four hours. I'll tell you more when we do the full autopsy," Darzi said as his assistants loaded the body inside their van. "There was no phone, just a wallet in his pocket and a gun inside his waistband."

He held up two evidence bags. The gun was a stainless steel 1911 Colt Commander. The grips had an outline of the state of Texas with a gold star in the middle. He hadn't even tried to draw his gun. For some reason, he had felt that he was safe. Had he specifically picked the parking lot of the sheriff's office to meet someone?

Darlene walked up beside me. "Was that our Texas Ranger?"

"I'm afraid so."

"Then I think we can move forward with the working hypothesis that the same person who killed Todd killed the Ranger."

"Did he know or suspect that he was meeting the killer?" I asked rhetorically.

"Why didn't he take more precautions?" she asked, and I floated my idea that he thought meeting in the parking lot would be safe enough.

"Maybe it was just bad luck on the Ranger's part that he parked back here. The killer comes in knowing enough to look for cameras, sees that he's in luck and takes advantage," Darlene suggested.

"Or it was some of that good luck that bad guys

sometimes have, like the fact the Zodiac Killer was probably stopped by police, but they had the wrong witness description."

"By the way, Maxwell said for us to call him when we don't have a dead body in the parking lot," Darlene said

"Ass."

"He can be."

"We could give him hell if we wanted. He's reported two of the three murders."

"You've got a point. I've heard Maxwell say that one of the first people you need to look at is the guy who finds the body," Darlene said, smiling a little at the irony.

"I'd need a motive. Has he ever been to Texas? For that matter, were either of our first two victims ever in Texas?"

"That's a starting point. We need to run down our suspect list and double-check alibis for all three murders. Of course, just because the crimes are connected doesn't mean that we're dealing with just one killer. Maybe Winter killed the first two and then someone else killed Winter," Darlene speculated. One of the things I liked about working with her was her flexible mind.

"It's unlikely, but at this point I guess we need to be open to any theory."

There was nothing else of interest in the car—no laptop or tablet. It was a rental and I'd have to call the company to tell them that they were going to lose the use of it for a while, possibly years. Of course, with all of the blood inside of it, they'd probably prefer that the insurance company just write them a check.

I called Lorraine Bell and asked her if she knew where Winter was staying. Turned out that he was staying in the same motel in Tallahassee that she and her mother were. I debated whether to tell her about Winter's murder over the phone, but decided I'd break the news when I went over there to search his room. I told Lorraine that I'd be by around two o'clock.

Darlene agreed to stay and keep an eye on the crime

scene. Before I left, I checked in with Major Parks, who'd already had dispatch send a text to all of the deputies who'd worked last night and asked them to secure their body cams and come in for interviews as possible witnesses. I was pretty sure that even the ones who had gone home to sleep this morning had already heard that a body had been found in our parking lot. The department ran a very efficient grapevine.

I met with the day manager of the motel, who was very interested to hear that one of his guests had met with a bad end. He was in his late thirties and wearing a tactical 501 belt and duty shoes. I wondered if he had dreams of being a security guard.

"What happened to him?" he asked eagerly. "Was he into drugs? I'm pretty sure there's a lot of that going on here. I've called the Tallahassee police a couple of times when things have gotten out of hand. I know one of the sergeants pretty well. He lives in my apartment complex."

I listened attentively and nodded. I wasn't really interested in his bromance with a police sergeant, but I wanted to get whatever information I could out of him. Nosey old ladies and guys who were wannabe cops could often be our biggest pains in the ass, but also the best sources of information.

"I'm glad a guy like you is on the desk. I want you to think back. Did Mr. Winter do anything unusual or have any odd friends come by?

"Gee, I don't know. I can't really see his room from the front desk. I know he was a pretty friendly guy. I'd see him talking to just about anyone. You know, not just the girls. Let me think about it."

"That would be great. If you come up with anything, give me a call." I gave him one of my cards. He held the embossed sheriff's investigator card like it was a hundred-dollar bill.

"I'll ask the other staff too."

As he walked with me to Winter's room, he asked me what I was looking for. I told him I was just doing an informal once-over to see if there was anything that demanded immediate attention, such as another dead body. I shouldn't have said that because it just made him want to come in and look too.

"You should wait in the hall," I told him. "Evidence."

He nodded earnestly, letting me know that he understood.

I was happy to see that Winter had left a "do not disturb" sign on the door handle. The manager opened the door and stood well back per my instructions. A quick look around told me that there wasn't a body hiding under the bed. I found Winter's suitcase and a carry-on bag and poked through them quickly, just to make sure there wasn't anything obviously time sensitive. I doubted if our techs would be able to make it over there today. There was no laptop, tablet or phone in the room, which suggested that they'd probably been in the car and the killer had taken them.

I took one last look around, doubting that the killer had ever been in the room. I put crime scene tape across the door and reminded the eager beaver manager that he had my card so he could call me if he saw anything out of the ordinary, like someone lurking around the grounds.

Next I went to the Bells' room. Both women looked older and more dejected than the first time I'd seen them. I hated to tell them about Winter. I knew that they were relying on him to bring them some measure of peace. Lorraine sat down hard on the bed when I delivered the news, while her mother, Rita, turned to stone as I watched. Her face hardened and turned an ash grey that unnerved me.

"How is that possible?" Lorraine asked, her hands balled into fists in her lap.

"I promise you that we're going to find out," was all I could tell her. I couldn't tell her that I thought the two murders were connected because it was only a suspicion, and one that could have very well turned out to be completely wrong.

"He must have been onto something. He'd found the murderer and was killed for what he knew," Rita said as though she were the Greek chorus in this tragedy.

"That's one of a number of possibilities."

"That man. The deputy who fought with my grandson. Mr. Winter was killed at his place of work," she continued, now a prosecuting attorney making her opening statement.

"We still have a lot of investigating to do before we'll have any answers."

"Do you want to find the killer?" Rita asked, piercing me with her stony eyes.

"Not only do I want to, we *will* find him," I said, trying to assure myself as much as them.

I called Darlene on my way back to the office and we discussed bringing Landon in to look at the latest case. She said she'd give him a call.

Landon pulled into the office parking lot right behind me. We shook hands and walked back to where Shantel and the other techs were finishing up with the car.

"This is a very mature killer," he said, looking around the parking lot and back at the building. "To have had the nerve to meet this guy at the back of the sheriff's office parking lot and then to stab him."

"And apparently he managed to do it without being caught on the security cameras," I told him as we walked up beside Darlene, who was watching the clean up.

"They're almost done. The tow truck is on its way to move the car," she said, nodding to Landon. "You can walk up and take a look at it."

Landon and I both walked to the car. This was the first opportunity that I'd had to take a close look at the scene. Winter had bled a lot, but since his heart had stopped almost immediately, he didn't bleed out. The keys were still in the ignition and he had backed the car into the space.

"Why'd he park back here?" Landon mused. "Did he know he was meeting with the killer? And did the killer specify where he should park for the meeting? Or did the victim decide on meeting here? It almost seems too unlikely that the victim just happened to pick a spot where your surveillance cameras wouldn't pick them up. Maybe he didn't want to be caught on camera any more than the killer."

"Winter obviously underestimated the threat that the murderer posed to him," I said.

"Did the killer arrive here in a car?"

"We haven't reviewed all the footage, but I doubt it. He probably parked a block over and came up to the back of our property here. You can make almost the whole walk in the shadows of trees and bushes," Darlene, who'd been listening to us, chimed in. "I walked it. I've already asked the businesses over on the other street to provide us with any of their CCTV footage."

"We're pretty sure that this is related to the Harper case, at least," I said.

"This murder wasn't a part of his larger plan," Landon said thoughtfully. "In the other cases, he stalked his victims and attacked them from one of their blind spots. Here, he was forced to attack at a time, place and with a method that left him much more vulnerable to the whims of fate. If he gets away with this one, he was lucky as well as careful."

"I see what you mean. The other two were easy by comparison."

"Exactly. This one was dangerous. He was facing an adversary who was aware of his presence, was capable of defending himself and had chosen a place that, by itself, presented challenges."

"He risked a lot to murder Winter."

"Exactly. He murdered this man not because he had a desire to kill him, but because he had to," Landon said.

"Then the question becomes why," Darlene noted.

"I'll go over what I have so far and give you an updated profile. I can tell you that this narrows the age range some.

He has to be at least thirty. I'm not sure about the upper limit. Maybe the killer's pretty old and that caused Winter to let his guard down. You said the man was a retired Texas Ranger?"

"That's right."

"He might have gotten cocky, thinking that the killer would only risk killing people that he could blindside."

"Winter didn't seem arrogant or careless," I said.

"Clearly he made some miscalculation." Landon indicated the car with the blood-covered seat. I couldn't argue the point.

After Landon had left and the car had been towed the few hundred feet to our impound lot, Darlene and I sat down with Lt. Johnson. He wasn't happy.

"Do I even need to tell you that this is a high-priority case?" he asked. "This department needs you two to come up with answers. Now. A body in the parking lot is bound to affect morale," he said without any attempt to be funny.

"We're pretty sure that this murder is related to our two cases," I said.

"Pretty sure? Those are not words that instill confidence. We need you to be positive, certain. We're going to be looking for a damn guarantee." With his dark mocha skin tone, it was hard to tell, but I was pretty sure that the blood was rushing to his head.

"Okay, push us and I'd say that we're certain the cases are connected."

"You have evidence?"

"No, not really," I said meekly. I wondered if Dad had put him up to this dress-down or if it was his own idea. He was almost as good at it as Dad was.

"Bring me the bastard that did this, along with an armload of evidence. And be quick about it."

"Honestly, this is a complicated case that's going to require—"

"Time. Something you don't have much of. If you aren't up to this, then say so now. I'll replace you in a minute," he said. Clearly, he wasn't worried about *my* morale.

"I'm good. Yes, sir."

"Deputy Marks, what about you? Are you up to the challenge?"

"Yes, sir."

"I do have a request," I said, risking Johnson's wrath. He stared at me with eyes that dared me to make it. "I'd like for the restriction regarding Darlene working on the Baxter case to be lifted."

I held my breath while I waited to see if I had brought the furies of hell down upon myself. Johnson took his eyes off of me long enough to look at Darlene. I can only assume he was assessing her trustworthiness.

"Done. But," he held up a finger, "Henley is still on leave and is not to be involved in the investigations in any way. Is that understood?"

"Yes, of course," I said, knowing that Johnson would see to it that I received a very harsh punishment if he found out just how much I'd already involved Pete.

"I want a report in two days on where this investigation stands and where it's going. Good hunting," he said, dismissing us.

Once we were far enough from his office that there wasn't a danger of being heard, I turned to Darlene. "You shouldn't have spoken up so much in there," I said sarcastically.

"And maybe you should have poked the bull a couple more times," she shot back with an equal amount of snark.

CHAPTER SIXTEEN

Darlene and I took over the conference room, spreading out all the reports and files that we had on the murders. I called Cara before we got started with our latest review.

"I'm going to be here for a while."

"I heard." There was sympathy in her voice and I could tell she understood the possible fallout of the latest murder.

"Were you going to come over?"

"I hadn't planned to, but I can."

"It'd be great if you went over and fed Ivy."

"And have something warm for you when you get home?"

"I can take that a lot of different ways," I joked and almost felt like smiling.

"Take it any way you want. I'll have some chili on the stove."

After I hung up, Darlene looked at me from across the conference table. "You know, if she moved into your place your life would be a lot simpler."

I wondered if that was true. I thought about asking Darlene when she'd last had someone living with her, but something about Darlene had always made me shy away from asking too many personal questions.

"Maybe," I said vaguely.

We laid out the information we had on our few suspects—Pete, Maxwell and Dereck. Though I still felt stupid calling Pete a suspect. I made a list of the pros and cons for each of them, while Darlene dug deeper into Winter's background, including locating his next of kin and informing them of his death.

I called Dereck to get some additional background information directly from him. After having been lied to once, I planned on verifying everything he told me with at least one other source.

"Where were you born?" I started.

"Why?" He already sounded concerned.

"We just need to fill out our report."

"You need my birthplace?"

"I'm going to be honest with you, Dereck. We're going to thoroughly look into your background. We weren't lying when we told you that we're only interested in the murders, but after you neglected to tell us everything you knew about Mrs. Baxter the first time, we have to check you out," I said in my best school principal voice.

"Columbus, Georgia," he said, sounding resigned.

"Have you ever been to Texas?"

There was a long pause. Finally, "Why?"

"I thought we'd gotten past that. I've explained this to you. We have a whole list of things we're checking out. I'm not going to explain the reason for each question. Even if I was inclined to do that, which I'm not, some of them have to do with parts of the case that I can't reveal."

"Yeah, I've been to Texas. I lived there for three years. My dad was in the Army and was stationed at Fort Hood."

So there *was* a Texas connection. "How old were you?"

"It was my last year in junior high through my second year of high school."

That was old enough to get into some serious trouble. Had he done something that brought him to the attention of a Texas Ranger? I'd done a basic background check on him and hadn't turned up anything. However, it wouldn't have included events for which he was only questioned, or for anything he was charged for as a juvenile.

"Were you ever involved in any crimes while you were in Texas?"

"Like what?"

I thought that was an odd response. "Like anything that involved law enforcement officers."

"No, I was never arrested or anything. I got stopped by the cops for speeding once and another time I was in a traffic accident."

"Was anyone seriously hurt in the accident?"

"No, not really. The woman driving the other car was banged up a little. The accident was ruled as no fault." He threw in the last point rather quickly. I made a note to get in touch with the Texas DMV and pull any records they had on the accident.

"You were never questioned regarding any serious crime?"

"No."

"Have you ever heard of a Texas Ranger named Steve Winter?" There was a long pause on the other end of the phone. Was he just taking my question seriously and trying to remember, or was he trying to come up with a lie to keep me from discovering the truth?

"No. I don't think so."

He said he was at home Sunday night, and David and Anna were still keeping their distance, so he didn't have an alibi for Winter's murder. I asked a few more basic questions, then had him give me the names of some of his relatives and friends so I could verify everything he'd told me.

Chief Maxwell was a little easier to research since he had a rèsumè several places online, including his candidate website. There was nothing about Texas on his website, but then again, it didn't mention his expensive private college education either. He preferred to downplay his privileged background in favor of his good ol' boy routine.

I found his LinkedIn profile, which spelled out all of his education and training in tedious detail. Looking through his work experience, I found no gaps. Not a single one. Which seemed a bit suspicious in and of itself. Who manages to never be out of work or out of school from the time they enter kindergarten? Surely somebody had fired the jerk at some point. I sent some emails and called a few people, trying to find someone who knew him well enough to tell tales out of school, as my granddad used to say.

Two hours later, Darlene and I compared notes.

"Dereck is looking better all the time. He was in Texas for several years. I've sent several emails to law enforcement agencies around Fort Hood, asking if they had any contact with Dereck which wouldn't have been reflected in his record. As for Maxwell, it's going to take a while to dig down into his past. On the surface, there's no indication that he and Winter were ever in the same state until recently. But with them both being in law enforcement, they could have met at a conference or training seminar," I finished with a shrug.

"Okay, well, I talked to Winter's ex-wife, Sandra. He has some cousins, but no other relatives. His parents died almost a decade ago, and he didn't have any siblings. Sandra said she'd take care of the burial arrangements. Apparently, they got along even after the divorce. According to Sandra, she just needed a husband who gave a damn about something other than putting bad guys in jail."

"Seems odd that a man who was that dedicated to his work would have retired at his age."

"Sandra said that had surprised her too. When he told her, she contacted some friends who still worked with the Rangers and they said that he was asked to resign. He'd become obsessed with unsolved crimes and wouldn't take no for an answer."

"Did she know anything about the cases that he was obsessed with?"

"No, but she gave me the names of a couple of his Ranger buddies that she thought would be more than glad to help us."

"An obvious assumption would be that he came here because of one of those cases."

"That's what Sandra figures. She said that leaving the Rangers wouldn't have stopped him if he was determined to follow a lead. She made him sound pretty bullheaded."

"That was my impression too."

"At least we have a possible motive for Winter's murder."

"Whoever he'd been chasing turned on him. The hunter became the hunted."

"Odd that he was caught flatfooted."

"My impression was that he was a very straightforward kind of guy. The way he was killed broke our perp's pattern. Winter might not have considered his quarry that flexible."

"Never underestimate your enemy."

"That's something we need to keep in mind when we get close to this guy."

"Agreed, Rookie," she said, clearly implying that if anyone was going to let their guard down, it would be me.

"Don't worry about me," I said, doing my best tough-guy impression.

We spent another couple of hours trying to develop either more suspects or more motives for Harper's or Baxter's murders. It was nine o'clock when I looked at my watch. "We aren't getting anywhere. There isn't enough data."

"Agreed. I'll tackle the Ranger contacts tomorrow."

"And I'll follow up with Parks on the car and body cams."

When I finally made it home, I was comforted by the smell of chili on the stove as much as by the kiss that Cara greeted me with. Alvin and Ivy were sleeping on the couch, curled up next to each other. *Is this a sign that Cara and I should give the cohabitation thing a chance?* the romantic part of my brain asked, while the practical part told me that only an idiot would see a sign in the random behavior of pets.

On my way into work Tuesday morning, I wondered if a trip out to Texas would help. *Dad's budget would love that*, I thought. He'd probably make me set up a GoFundMe site instead.

I called Maxwell to reschedule our meeting.

"Are there going to be any more dead bodies in the parking lot?" he asked me snidely.

"I know. We should be more like your department and bury them in the basement."

"All of my skeletons are firmly locked in the closet," he said, obviously not thinking about how that might sound to a man who was investigating him for murder. "Just kidding, of course. I'll be there at ten," he added rather lamely.

Darlene and I considered our options as we waited for Maxwell in the conference room.

"Winter is the case that we have the best chance of cracking," I said.

"Exactly. Like Landon told us, the killer committed that murder because he had to. There's a link between him and Winter. We just have to find it."

"Deep in the heart of Texas," I mused.

"Don't go getting poetic on me. I called the Rangers' headquarters in Austin and left messages for the ones that Sandra said were friends of Winter's."

We seemed to have run out of things to say. I looked at my watch and we still had fifteen minutes before Maxwell was scheduled to arrive.

"You know, you don't have to be here for the interview. I can ask Johnson to come down. We were all set to go that way yesterday before we found the body."

"No, I'm okay with it. Now that I've been given permission to be on the case, I *want* to be on the case. Maxwell helped me out by giving me a job with the police department. He's a smart guy and was professionally supportive. But he's a suspect and I'm good with that. Do I think he did it? No. But I think if we were honest, we'd all admit that we seldom go into an interview without some opinion about the suspect. Even when it's someone you don't know, how are you going to keep your mind from assessing their clothing, their appearance and their attitude, then creating a bias for or against them? The only thing you can do is be aware of it and not let it influence your decisions."

"Wow. Nice lecture. You should teach a class at the academy," I joked and she shot me a bird.

There was a light knock on the door and Maxwell walked in.

"They said you all were in here." He looked less composed than yesterday, which was funny since that was just after he'd found a dead body.

"Have a seat," I said. Darlene got up and moved to my side of the table so we were both facing Maxwell.

"Marks," Maxwell said in greeting to her as she moved past him. She just nodded. Clearly he was trying to establish her as a friend in the room. Equally clear was her gentle rebuff.

I gave him the usual song and dance about recording the interview and the fact that he was joining us of his own free will. He looked down at the table, then over at us.

"Nice of you all not to do this in one of your interview rooms."

As the chief of police, he knew the layout of the sheriff's office almost as well as I did. The two departments worked closely together on any criminal activity that took place within the city limits. It was a credit to both Dad and Maxwell that they could have a professional working relationship, even though neither of them liked the other. This wasn't always the case. Give me half a day and I could come up with a hundred examples where personal animosities between the heads of two law enforcement agencies had meant that bad guys went free and good people suffered.

"Where were you on the night of April sixteenth and the early morning hours of April seventeenth?"

"The night that the Harper boy was killed? I was at home asleep. I worked on some material for my campaign and went to bed around midnight. My wife was out of town, so there is no one who can confirm my whereabouts. You could check the pings from my cell phone, but all that would mean is that I left my cell phone at my house."

"Had you ever met Todd Harper?"

"Not to my knowledge, but this is a small town. I wouldn't be surprised if I'd bumped into him somewhere. I'm excellent with names, so I can say with some certainty that I didn't get introduced to him formally or informally."

I thought that gave him a little wiggle room if someone had seen them together, but overall, it was pretty definitive. I read off Todd's address. "Have you ever been to that address?"

"Funny you should ask. I was there about five years ago for a domestic dispute. One of my officers had responded to an argument called in by a neighbor. When the officer attempted to separate the couple, he was struck by the man and beaten almost unconscious. He was fortunate to have a stun gun on his belt that he was able to deploy. I was called to the scene because of the injured officer and the need for a use of force report. The officer, it was Wade by the way, was so pumped with adrenaline and terrified for his own life that he just kept hitting the guy with the stun gun. Wade almost killed him."

"That was the only time you were at that address?"

"Yes."

Moving on, I thought. "Let's talk about Texas." I'd decided to throw it out that way just to see his reaction. To my surprise, I saw a flash in his eyes and, for just a second, they darted right and left. He quickly regained his composure, but he'd obviously been surprised. He thought I already knew something about him and Texas and now I wasn't going to

165

give up until I found out what it was.

"What about Texas?" he asked casually, but it was too late.

"I want to know about your connection with Texas."

"I don't know what you mean." What he did not say was: *I have never been to Texas nor do I have any connections with Texas.*

"I mean that I want to know about the time you spent in Texas." I decided to cast the dice and see what happened. If he'd never been in Texas and the link between him and the state involved something a bit more tenuous, then I'd just shown him that I was fishing. But he frowned.

"How is that pertinent to your investigation?" More stalling.

"Are you saying you don't want to answer the question?" Darlene threw at him.

He looked startled that she was still there.

"No, no, I didn't say that. But before I lay all my personal business on the table, I want to make sure that there's a point to this line of questioning."

"There is," I said bluntly. "You understood before you walked in here how this would work."

I wondered if pushing him was the right move. My ace in the hole was the fact that, in the middle of an election campaign, he didn't want to be seen as hiding anything. And while he could be reasonably sure that we wouldn't purposefully leak any information, he couldn't afford to piss us off too badly and put our honor to the test. I could almost hear the gears turning in his head as he weighed all the pros and cons.

"Okay, I can't imagine what this has to do with your current investigations, but I was in Texas years ago for approximately six months. Back in 1989."

"Are you going to make us pry the answers from you?" I asked.

He knew what we wanted and, now that he'd opened the door, there'd be no closing it.

"What the hell. Okay, I ran off to get married. Her name

was Este Cantrell. I met her at Emory. Well, I was at Emory and she was working as a waitress in Atlanta. She was from Texas. I was an idiot and fell in love with her. My parents hated her. Este didn't care if I finished college or not and, after falling in love with her, I didn't either. Bottom line, she got pregnant. She went home to her mother without telling me. I followed her there with the intention of getting her to marry me. However, once we were in Texas, she had a different attitude toward me. Her parents didn't like me any more than my parents liked her. And Este was a daddy's girl.

"We were saved a lot of grief when she lost the baby. I stayed in Texas for a couple months after the miscarriage, but I was just hiding out from my parents." He stopped and then gave me a small smile. "The victim yesterday was a Texas Ranger. Stupid of me, I should have realized. You're looking for a link between me and the dead Ranger. Ha! Good luck."

"His name was Steve Winter. Ring any bells?" I asked.

"No, though, as good as my memory for names is, if I had met him more than twenty-five years ago, I probably wouldn't remember. And that's not wiggle room. Just the honest truth." He came across more sincere then I'd ever seen him.

We covered a little more ground with him, but couldn't find anything that excluded him or pointed directly at him. Maxwell left and we decided to ask Pete to come in for another interview. I called him and he was more than willing. I think he just wanted to spend some time in the office.

CHAPTER SEVENTEEN

I was sitting at my desk when Pete came in. Everyone who saw him waved, shook his hand or patted him on the back.

"Good seeing you in the office," I told him.

"Good to be here. I just wish all of this was cleared up. I was supposed to meet with Major Parks yesterday, but he got tied up trying to sort through all the cam footage and everything."

Pete, Darlene and I went into the conference room. We weren't going to treat him any differently than the other suspects and witnesses. We started the interview testing his alibi for the night of Winter's murder. Pete was home with his family, but only his wife could vouch for him during the time of the murder. No surprises there.

"Pete, have you ever been to Texas?"

"Drove through there once on my way to San Diego. My brother was in the Navy and he was stationed out there. Drove back through, too, of course. But those were the only times I've ever been in the state."

"When was this?"

"Let me think… Must have been 1995. I'm pretty sure about that, but I'll check."

"Did you have any interactions with law enforcement

while you were in the state?"

"No, no speeding tickets or anything like that. I guess you're looking for a tie in with the Texas Ranger. I don't think there is any. My trip through the Lone Star State was uneventful. In fact, I'd say it was downright boring."

Good, I thought. I'd already submitted the three suspects we had to the Texas Rangers so that they could check their records. Usually, I wouldn't have been very confident that another state's law enforcement agency would have the time or inclination to dig deep into their back cases, but when I'd mentioned that my call related to the murder of an ex-Ranger, I could hear them take notice on the other end of the phone.

We asked a few more questions, trying to be tough on Pete, but the effort felt false. *Because it is*, I admitted to myself. I just couldn't take him seriously as a suspect. I could sense the same feeling in Darlene as she attempted to put on her tough-girl act without a lot of luck.

"Are we done?" I asked Darlene after a while.

"We're done."

"I'll walk you out," I told Pete.

Once we were outside and out of earshot of any other deputies, I said, "I'm going to ask Dad to push Major Parks to move on your suspension. With luck, you'll get time served. We need you back."

"I appreciate that. I want to find out who put me in the crosshairs. I'm pretty disgusted with myself for letting it get me down. To say nothing of letting us do something very foolish," he finished under his breath.

"Let's hope we can get through that little brushfire without burning our asses," I said, feeling as paranoid as he looked.

I saw him off and was headed back toward the building when my phone rang.

"Hey, is this Investigator Macklin?"

Every time I get a call like that I start thinking about all of the cards I've handed out. "It is. How can I help you?"

"This is Martin from the motel. You gave me your card and told me to call if I remembered anything odd about that guy that was killed," he said, capturing my full attention. It was probably nothing more than investigational white noise, but at this point I was willing to listen to anything.

"What have you got?" I didn't find it hard to sound interested.

"I talked to one of the other managers, and he remembered a short old guy talking to the dead guy a couple of times. But that's not all. He said that one time they almost looked like they were getting into an argument."

"Did you ever see them talking?"

"I remember seeing them in the lobby a couple of days before the guy ended up dead. They looked at each other kinda funny."

"Kinda funny how?"

"The short dude kinda glared at the dead guy. And the dead guy, like, shook his head. Like it was sad or something. Oh, but now guess what?" he added eagerly.

"What?"

"The short guy isn't coming out of his room."

I was all interest again. "Not at all?"

"I ain't seen him. The night manager said he thought he saw him, like, sneak out to his car, drive off, come back and run to his room."

"Okay, listen, don't talk to anyone else. I'm coming over there now. Got it?"

"Yeah, cool, sure."

I hurried back inside and found Darlene typing up a report on one of the interviews.

"I think we may have another suspect," I said out of an abundance of confidence in the little tidbit the goofball manager had given me. I filled Darlene in.

"You know that's probably crap," she said. "But so is everything else we have. Let's go. You can drive."

My buddy was at the front desk and he was perfectly willing

to ignore a poor traveler trying to check in to come talk to me about his suspect.

After a five-minute discourse on how hard he'd worked to develop this lead, he gave us the guest's name and room number. His description of the guest was that he was about 5'6", maybe sixty-five years old, with grey, receding hair and a slightly stooped posture. This didn't make him sound like your average axe murderer.

We went up two floors and a couple doors down the hall. I didn't think our new suspect warranted drawn guns, so I just knocked on the door and stood where he could see me through the peephole.

"Who is it?" came a shaky voice from the other side of the door.

"Sheriff's deputy. Are you Fred Reeves?" I asked, holding up my star to the peephole. I didn't go into the fact that we weren't in our jurisdiction. That seemed a little nuanced for a peephole conversation.

"Go away." He sounded more scared than angry.

"We can't do that," I lied.

"Please," he moaned pathetically. Who was this guy?

"Just open the door and let us talk with you. If you are in trouble, maybe we can help." I threw in this last bit because, honestly, he sounded like he needed help.

The door opened to the end of the security latch. "Let me see your badge again. Hers too," he snapped.

We displayed our badges to the glasses peering out of the crack. When he was satisfied, the door opened wide.

"Go ahead, come in," he said, resigned. We followed him into a standard motel room. Only one of the beds had been slept in. The room was actually quite neat for a guy hiding out in a motel.

He slumped down in a chair by the small table that was crammed into the corner of the room.

"We're here investigating the death of Steve Winter," I told him, not wanting to confuse the issue with the other two murders.

"Yeah, yeah," he said dismissively. "I figured." He was beginning to act like a suspect. Was he about to confess? He reminded me of some of the fugitives that I'd caught up with. Once confronted, they just gave up.

"How do you know Steve Winter?" Darlene asked.

"He killed my daughter."

Darlene and I were completely unprepared for that surprising answer, but sometimes you have to go where the train takes you.

"When did he kill your daughter?"

"Fifteen years ago in Texas."

"Was he tried for the murder?" I asked, although having done a background check on him and having talked with the Texas Rangers since his murder, I knew that wasn't possible.

"Hell no, he wasn't tried. They weren't going to try one of their own. You should know that, you're one of them." Anger flashed in his eyes.

I began to believe that it was entirely possible that he could have killed Winter. He had a better motive than any of our other suspects.

"How did he kill her?" Darlene asked.

It was a good question. It was possible that he could have done something in the line of duty that inadvertently caused the death of Reeves's daughter. One of the hazards of making life-and-death decisions on a regular basis is that you are going to occasionally make the wrong one and innocent people can be hurt. You chase a dangerous suspect and hit a pedestrian who didn't see you coming. Or you have to choose which person to pull from a wrecked car that's sinking or burning because you only have time to save one. I could see Winter causing someone's death through no fault of his own, but rather a decision that had to be made.

"He killed her with a baseball bat. Sound familiar?" Reeves said disdainfully, blowing my theory out of the water in the process.

"Why do you think he killed your daughter?" I asked.

"Because he didn't like her. He was her coach and they'd

gotten into an argument about whether she should play in a game or not. Everyone saw them. I… I hate to say it, but Linda had a temper and, while they were arguing, she struck him. I saw his face. He was angry. Real angry."

"And you think that was enough motive for him to have killed your daughter?"

"You didn't see him. After it happened, he told me he was going to see to it that she didn't play anymore. I told him he couldn't kick her off of the team. I thought he was going to hit me, but he got all cold and said that we'd see what he could do. Damn near everyone at the game heard him say she'd never play on his team again. Of course, Linda was real upset. That night she left the house. Said she was going for a walk. I figured she'd go down to the field and hit balls. Linda would do that when she was mad."

He paused and I could tell that this was all as fresh in his mind as the day it had happened. "When she didn't come home, her mother and I went looking for her. We found her in the dugout."

"She'd been attacked?"

"No sexual assault, nothing like that. Just hit in the head with a baseball bat." He spoke the words with a cadence and tone that let me know he'd explained all of this a thousand times.

"Winter didn't have an alibi?" Darlene asked.

"Of course he had an alibi. A neighbor heard him inside his apartment. But that could have been anyone. The cops didn't want to arrest him. He was one of theirs."

"Okay. So you think he killed your daughter. Is that why you're here?" I asked.

"Of course. I've kept track of him ever since he did it. You think I'm going to let him get away with murder? And then… he killed someone else here. I *know* he killed that boy. Baseball bat, just like Linda. I should have killed him back in Texas."

Were we getting to a confession? Could this man have stabbed Winter through the heart? It would take nerve and speed and a bit of strength. The nerve could have been supplied by anger and this man had plenty of that.

We took down all the particulars of his daughter's murder. Something else for me to check with the Rangers.

"Where were you on Sunday night and early Monday morning?" Darlene asked.

"I didn't kill him. I wish I did, but I didn't. I was here and there wasn't anyone with me." Reeves looked lost, an Ahab without his whale.

We asked to search his room and he consented readily enough. We didn't find anything out of the ordinary. The laptop and phone that were in the room appeared to belong to the old man.

"Who do you think killed Winter?" I asked him.

"I expect it's a family member of someone he killed. Or maybe it was someone he was going to kill," Reeves answered.

There seemed to be no doubt in his mind that Winter was a stone-cold killer. Had he just spent so many years believing it that nothing would ever change his mind?

Then something occurred to me. "Do you know for sure that Winter was in this area when the first murder happened?"

The old man sighed. "I don't know. He was driving around the southeast, I know that. I use a clipping service... well, that's what they used to call it, but now everything is on the dang computer. But I saw an article about the murder, and that there was a baseball bat, so I got interested. I started calling all the hotels in the area and lo and behold if Mr. Winter ain't here in town," he said with a generous portion of venom.

Reeves agreed to give us his fingerprints and a DNA sample, so I waited with him while Darlene went down to the car to get the print and DNA collection kits.

"Did he suffer?" Reeves asked.

"Not long," I told him

"Shame. The pathologist said that my Linda wasn't killed

outright. She managed to rally and tried to crawl for help."

I wondered if Reeves had ever come to a point in his life after the murder of his daughter where he could have chosen to move on. Or had he been destined from the moment she was killed to go down a path that would lead him to lose everything he still had? If there *had* been a choice, I doubt he'd recognized it for what it was.

"I sorry for the loss of your daughter."

"You have no idea what I lost. She was amazing."

Darlene returned and we collected his prints and a DNA swab. As we were leaving, I shook his hand and told him not to leave the area without telling us first. His handshake was firm and strong. He could have plunged that knife into Winter.

"What do you think?" I asked Darlene when we were back in the car.

"Winter killed Harper and Baxter and then Reeves killed Winter. I don't know. It's nice and neat, but I can't quite see it. And if we could prove that Winter wasn't in the area when Harper was killed, then that would put a big hole in the theory."

"I've got the paperwork going to get us Winter's phone records. We can get ping data that might solve that much of the mystery. Though by eliminating that theory, we just put ourselves back at the beginning with three suspects that we don't like for the crimes."

"For each of the first two victims, we have multiple people who wouldn't mind seeing them dead. But the only problem is that the two sets don't have many people in common."

"Maybe we should go back to looking at three individual murders with three individual killers."

"That doesn't feel right either."

Without solving a damn thing, we pulled into the hospital parking lot. I'd called Dr. Darzi and convinced him that, since we were going to be in town, he should shuffle his schedule around and do the autopsy on Winter this afternoon.

"You know, my job is not to save you gasoline," he said good-naturedly when we entered the autopsy room. "But I guess I can help you out, since you're regular customers and all."

"How do you stay in such a good humor?" I asked, looking at Winter's body laid out on the stainless steel table.

"Death surrounds me. I had to learn to embrace it. The biggest fear any of us have is dying, so once I conquered that, what is there to be unhappy about? Being a coroner is a lot like being a Hindu swami," he said with a laugh.

The knife was still sticking in Winter's chest. "I was able to get a preliminary ID on the weapon," Darzi said.

"Looks like a commando knife."

"Give that man a prize. From comparing the handle, I'd say that it's specifically a British commando knife. Let's remove it and see if it is the real deal or a reproduction. I did a quick look online and both are easily obtainable," he said, reaching out and pulling on the knife. There was no sound, but the skin pulled apart sickeningly as he extracted the blade.

Darzi examined the goo on the blade carefully and took a couple of swabs for testing before wiping the blade clean.

"I'd say that this is an original. Twenty dollars and up. Available online and shipped directly to your house."

"Wonderful," I grumbled. Our only hope of matching the knife to the owner would be if the DNA swabs Shantel had taken at the scene came back to someone. It always seemed like a cop-out to rely on the criminal being an idiot. Unfortunately, I didn't think our killer was stupid enough not to wear gloves.

After an hour of poking, prodding and slicing, Dr. Darzi stepped away from the body and took off his gloves.

"He was a healthy man who died from a dagger to the heart. Your killer was either skilled or lucky. The blade passed almost perfectly between the third and fourth ribs on his left side. There is just the tiniest nick on the fourth rib."

"How strong would someone need to be to stab a man like that?" Darlene asked, probably thinking of Reeves.

"With this blade, not very. It would be awkward to do it from the passenger seat, but, as you can see from the angle, the attacker had the knife in his right hand and probably crossed his own chest to plunge the blade into the victim. What he would need to have been is quick and decisive."

On our way back to Adams County, we looked for one good suspect.

"I like Reeves for Winter," I said. "It was a cold-blooded but very personal killing. And I can imagine that Winter wouldn't have been too scared of Reeves, but might have wanted to meet in the sheriff's office parking lot just to avoid any issues."

"My problem with it is that you have to assume that Reeves would take the time to find the one spot in the parking lot where the security cameras wouldn't pick them up. That also suggests that he chose the spot."

"Which is possible, and would have made sense to Winter because he knew that Reeves thought he was a killer. Where would you meet someone you thought was a homicidal maniac? At a sheriff's office."

"Maybe. So Winter killed the rest?"

"Maybe not. Winter might be innocent of the other crimes, including Reeves's daughter, but Reeves thought he was guilty and killed him. A case of mistaken identity."

"Great, now we're in a Hitchcock film. I don't like that because it still leaves us looking for one or two other killers."

"I can solve that problem. Reeves killed everyone. He's crazy as a loon, maybe caused by his daughter's death, and just goes on a killing spree. Winter suspects him and, *boom*, Reeves kills him."

"That gets the neat package award. But it's completely unbelievable."

"Wish I believed *any* of this."

"I know what you mean."

"We need more data to get a good answer. At least we have Reeves's DNA and fingerprints for Shantel to send off for comparison."

"I think one of the basic questions we should focus on is, what triggered Winter's killing? Was it opportunity or something else? Reeves has probably had many opportunities over the years. Why would he choose now?"

When we got back to the office, we went down to Shantel's desk and asked her and Marcus to review evidence collected so far. We also gave them the knife used on Winter.

"We could take it apart. Sometimes there is a serial number or a maker's mark on the tang," Marcus suggested. He was our resident sharp object expert. For a quiet guy, he had a real affinity for pocket knives, machetes, katana and all manner of other edged weapons. He had shown me his collection once when I was over at his house and I'd never looked at him quite the same way.

"If you can do it without damaging the knife. I guess there is always the possibility that you could discover some biological material under the hilt that traces back to the killer."

"I'll see if I can get the hilt off," Marcus said.

All three murders had been committed without leaving much trace evidence. I wondered if there was anything on the piece of bat that I had in my safe deposit box. I felt guilty, and rightly so, for holding it back.

CHAPTER EIGHTEEN

I headed home at six, planning to work on my reports for a couple of hours. Cara was there and had heated up soup for dinner. It smelled warm and inviting, but I really just wanted to spread out my notes and focus on the reports. If Cara moved in, I was going to have to learn how to relax and ignore her. Even when you live with someone, you still need your own personal time to work on a project or to relax and charge your batteries for another day out in the real world.

"A penny for your thoughts," Cara said as I sat at the table, eating my soup and gently nudging Ivy away.

"Not worth even that," I said and gave her a little smile.

"Thinking about the murders?"

"That and other things," I answered, half hoping that she wouldn't pursue the subject.

"Other things? Like what?"

"I'm probably too tired to talk about it tonight." I immediately realized that I'd fallen into at trap where now I *wouldn't* be able to not talk about my thoughts.

"Okay, now you know you can't leave it like that."

I picked up my empty bowl and took it to the sink, giving myself some time to think it through.

"I admit I was thinking about the moving-in situation." I

looked over at Cara and could tell that calling it a "situation" wasn't the best move. "I didn't mean it like that. I'm just trying to think about this from all angles." Again, I knew that I was making a mess of things. I sat back down at the table and took her hand.

"Whatever. I'm really not pushing it anymore," she said, sounding only a little miffed.

"I knew I shouldn't have brought this up. But I just keep thinking that I want us to be ready."

"Ready for what?" She tried to make her tone neutral, but failed.

"All of the little day-to-day stuff. That's all. I'm sure that you have days when you just want to come home from work and not… I don't know, be bothered by another person in the house." *Damn*, I thought, *that sounds insulting even to me.*

"I'm a bother?"

"No, no, you aren't. But I'm sure that *I* can be. Look, I'm not explaining myself well at all." I took a couple of seconds and tried to regroup. "I'm a guy. I do stupid guy things all the time. When you're around, I try to minimize the amount of dumb man stuff that I do."

At least this got the hint of a smile from her eyes. "You do plenty of stupid man stuff when I'm around," she said, making me think that I might yet be able to salvage this discussion.

"Exactly. But you don't know the half of it. If you're here all the time, you're going to have to put up with much worse. Leaving the toilet seat up, towels not hung up, clothes all over the bedroom floor, dirty dishes left in the sink. I have to really work at not being a disgusting pig when you're around. I know I won't be able to do it 24/7, 365 days a year." I tried to make a joke of it, but saying it out loud made me realize that there was a lot of truth in what I was saying.

"I'm sure you're right, but I won't be able to be the perfect woman either. You'll find feminine hygiene products in your trash, my hair will clog up the shower drain and I'll run the water the whole time I'm brushing my teeth. But that's what living together is all about. And it's okay. You know my parents. Hell, we lived at a nudist camp for three months once. I know all about bodily functions and all the other dark secrets of the reclusive human troll. Yes, there are going to be things that annoy each of us, but my loony mom would tell you that you should enjoy learning all the weird, crazy crap that makes up the person that you've fallen in love with. Knowing someone better than anyone else does is a gift that that person has entrusted to you."

I still wasn't convinced. "You make it sound like a very blending-of-souls, sparkly goodness sort of thing, but how will you feel if I come home one day and I'm in a pissy mood and letting all of my worst habits come to the surface?"

"Okay, I admit that one of the things I find really hard is to let someone be in a bad mood. That's on me. I guess that's something I'll have to work on. 'Cause you're right. You'll need space to be mad or sad or moody or depressed, whatever. I get it."

"And I appreciate the fact that you recognize that. We just need to make our relationship more about working on ourselves than it is about working on the other person." I was trying to make a final, epic statement that would enable me to exit the conversation while I was ahead.

"Yep. So what do you think?" she asked, blocking my exit.

I wanted to play stupid and say, "About what?" but I knew better. "I'm thinking about the possibility. Do I get points for that?" I asked hopefully.

"You do." She leaned forward and kissed me lightly on the lips. Wow. I'd managed to survive both the dreaded move-in conversation and the relationship conversation that it had morphed into.

I grabbed my laptop and dove quickly into my reports. How many days did I have left before I would have to give Cara a definite answer one way or the other? A week, maybe? I made a firm decision at that moment not to think about it.

I contacted the Texas Rangers to set up some phone interviews with folks who had known and worked with Winter. I was able to mix it up a bit, getting phone appointments with a woman who worked in the office, a man who'd been his supervisor and another guy who'd been his partner for a while. I thought that this group would be able to give me the best overall picture of Winter, as well as enable me to draw out as much personal history as possible from a thousand miles away. The Rangers also agreed to send me a copy of his personnel records. It had taken a while, but I was finally able to convince them that they could send the records without a warrant.

Darlene also spent the morning on the phone with Texas. She was looking into the Linda Reeves murder. It was going to be interesting to see where our two paths crossed.

I took my first phone interview with Sue Wylie, the woman who worked in records at the Rangers' office.

"I was sooooo sorry to hear about Steve. He was the nicest guy you could ever meet. Some of the fellows treat the staff like we don't count 'cause we don't carry guns. Not Steve. He knew everyone's name. Used to bring me a flower on my birthday, and he wasn't being mushy, he was just being kind. You know?"

I agreed with her that he had seemed like a nice guy. "How long did you know him?"

"He and I started here only a couple of months apart. So more than thirty years. My, it doesn't hardly seem possible. And now you say that someone killed him. That's horrible. Of course, he was fearless. Got in several gunfights while he was working as a Ranger. One time, he went out to some old trailer in the back country. Turned out it was a drug lab. He and his partner shot down six of them. Both Roger and Steve were hit. Thankfully, neither was hurt bad. Roger said that, after he was hit, Steve purposely put himself between the bad guys and Roger. Saved his life."

"Were there any cases that Steve wasn't able to solve? Something in particular that ate at him?" I asked and, for the first time since we started talking, there was silence at the other end of the line.

"There was," Sue said after a long pause. "Honestly, it caused him no end of trouble." She still seemed hesitant to give me the details.

"Whatever you can tell me might help us to catch the man who killed Steve. We think that there could be a link to one of his old cases," I encouraged her.

"That case just caused so much trouble around here." She sighed. "I hate dredging it all up. But if there's a chance that doing so will help catch Steve's killer..."

After another long pause, she told the story. "The murder happened when Steve was at the height of his career. It was a young girl. Linda... Reeves, yes, that's right. She was killed at a ballpark with a softball bat. But what was so horrible—not that the poor girl being killed wasn't horrible enough—but what made it so bad for Steve, was that she was on a softball team that he coached. There had been some trouble with her father before the murder. I mean, trouble between Steve and her father. So when the girl was killed, her father was sure that Steve had done it. Actually, more than a few people thought Steve might have been involved."

"But he was cleared?"

"Oh, yes, he had an alibi and, well, it was just ridiculous. But the department had to take it seriously. They took his life apart, but there wasn't a shred of evidence. And Steve never once tried to stall the investigation. He just stood back and let them go through everything in his past and present. There just wasn't anything to be found."

"I can see where Steve would be interested in finding the real killer."

"Not interested. Obsessed. I think it was two things. One, he knew the girl and had coached her. And, two, of course, the fact that until the murderer was found, there would always be that hint of suspicion that he had something to do with it. So I think everyone understood why Steve was working on the case and wouldn't let it go. But Steve—and I admire him and would never say a bad word about him—just went too far with it. Couldn't seem to concentrate on anything else after that. I mean, he did good work. Lord knows that Steve's worst work was a ton better than some people's best. But it just... got in the way, if you know what I mean."

"I'm not sure I do."

"I don't want to talk out of turn. You really should speak with some of the Rangers. They can tell you a lot more than me. And they know the inside stuff. I just heard office gossip. But I never passed it on. I respected Steve so much."

"Fair enough." I thanked her and told her I might need to speak with her again. I also promised that if we found the killer, I'd personally send her a text and let her know.

My next call was with Roger Thomas, a fellow Ranger and an ex-partner of Winter's. I wondered if it was the same Roger that Steve had defended in the gunfight Sue had mentioned. If so, I couldn't expect an unbiased opinion from him.

"Thomas here," said the voice on the other end of the phone, completely absent of any Texas drawl. I explained who I was and why I was calling.

"I hate it. Steve should be sitting here next to me right now, counting down the days until our retirement. I tried to tell him more than once that there were times you had to let the dead sleep. But his damned Texas stubbornness would have none of that. Nope. Had to go hunting for his elusive killer. Of course, if he was killed by the same phantom that he's been hunting then I guess he proved all of us wrong."

"We just don't know yet where the investigation is going to end up."

"Been there and done that. What can I do for you?"

I gave him the CliffsNotes version of how I had met Winter. "Now he's dead and we've discovered that he might have been here, not as a private detective hired by a victim's family, but rather as a man on his own hunt for a killer. Naturally, we are very interested in the person he was hunting."

"Did the prey turn on the hunter? I can tell you what I know. Of course, the investigation into Linda's murder is still open, so there's some information that I'll have to withhold."

"This is not a threat, but I'm prepared to get a warrant to look at your files."

"I understand. And that would be an interesting fight between Florida and Texas. But I don't think it will come to that. Just have your sheriff talk with some of our high-and-mightys. The case is frigid cold, so they'll probably be more than glad to fully cooperate with you. Though they'll most likely make you come out here to look at the files."

"If I have to do that, I'll probably have to pay for the plane ticket out of my own pocket."

"I hear you, brother," he sympathized. "Okay, I pulled the file and went over it first thing this morning. I remembered some of it, but the memory isn't what it used to be." He told me the same story as Sue.

"What was the argument that he had with the girl?"

"There was some debate about that. Steve always contended that he was trying to get her to be more of a team player. But her father said that Steve treated her differently than the other girls. He—and this is unsubstantiated—he stated that his daughter had rejected Steve's advances and so Steve retaliated by not playing her or putting her in positions that didn't show off her talents. Her father expected Linda to get a full scholarship to college. Softball isn't like football, but competition is competition."

"You didn't buy his allegations?"

"Not for a minute. I'd spent a whole bunch of time on the job with Steve. He hardly even looked at women, let alone girls. Other guys, yeah, they were real hound dogs. Steve, he just cared about catching bad guys. If you'd told me he'd had a wet dream, I'd expect it to be about bringing

down a drug gang. Even her father eventually changed his
story, said he wasn't sure that any of that was true."

"But you all investigated Steve?"

"With a passion. It was an easy decision to make, 'cause
we all knew there wouldn't be anything to find. We
interviewed almost every female he'd talked to in the ten
years prior to the murder. What we heard: perfect
gentleman, nicest man, best guy, wish he was single,
respectful, kind, and on and on."

"What about the allegation that he wasn't fair to Linda?"

"The rest of the team and the other parents backed up
Steve. Said that Linda was a hot dog and a hot head. Most
said that Steve had let her get away with too much."

"He had an alibi, right?"

"Yep, though if there had been any other evidence, I
don't think the alibi would have stopped a prosecution. It
was the wife, in bed, never left the house—that kind of alibi.
But the ballpark wasn't that far from the Winters' home, and
Steve was in great shape at the time. He could have found
time to meet Linda at the park and kill her, but combined
with everything else, it was a no-go."

"I know some investigators that keep a case open on
their desk, have the picture of the victim taped to the wall,
and go back to the cold case investigation whenever they
have time. I'd even say that some of them are obsessed. Why
was it such a big deal that Winter couldn't let it go?"

"I hear that. The trouble was, he tried to shoehorn his
killer into other cases. In a decade, I bet he tried to tie
Linda's killer to half a dozen other cases. The crazy thing
was that we had good suspects for most of those cases. He
pissed off prosecutors, investigators, sheriffs, district
attorneys, you name 'em and he made them mad.
Everywhere he looked, he saw his Machiavellian murderer
pulling the strings. No one could talk him out of it."

"Could he have been right?"

"I don't know. I spent two weeks once going over all of
his evidence. Used up my personal leave. I dug through

everything he had and, at the end of the day, all I could say was maybe. Possibly. And where Steve was concerned, I couldn't trust my own judgment. That man saved my life.

"We were in a firefight with a bunch of drugged-out rednecks with shotguns, AKs, Uzis, you name it. Our car looked like something out of the streets of Fallujah when it was over. I'd been hit in the arm and was trying to put a new magazine in my gun as this mountain of a tweeker was coming at me with a shotgun. I was praying and trying to load my gun, knowing that I didn't stand a chance, when Steve ran from cover and stood between me and the other guy. He put two rounds in the guy's off switch. Found out later Steve had already been shot in the leg when he did that.

"So you can understand that I wanted to believe him. I told everyone that I agreed with his conclusions. But I really just don't know. The evidence is fifty-fifty at best." He stopped, sounding tired.

"What were some of the cases he tried to connect to Linda's?"

"Let me think… There was one where, and this was odd, another law enforcement officer was the killer. A woman deputy from down near Austin. She and her husband had had a huge fight at a bar. A day later, her husband was found with a bullet to the back of his head. Her backup snubby was used in the shooting. She claimed that it had been stolen between the fight and the shooting. If I had a dime for every murderer whose gun was stolen before it was used to kill someone, I'd be rich. Steve claimed that the same guy who had killed Linda and pointed the finger at him was doing the same thing to this cop. He muddied the waters bad enough that the woman got a not guilty verdict.

"That was the case that was the last straw, and they pushed Steve until he resigned. Before that, um, there was a man—I think he was a prosecutor—who was accused of killing his neighbor because the neighbor was suing him for some arrest. I don't remember all the details. Anyway, there were more. But the point is, there wasn't any hard evidence that the cases were linked."

"Did anyone besides you take his ideas seriously?"

"The first couple of times, when Steve started pushing his theory, everyone was like: 'Steve knows what he's doing, so we'll go for it.' We put pressure on the locals to let us come in, and we did the full Monty on them. Nothing. Steve used the fact that there wasn't a lot of evidence to say it was proof that they *were* related. We tried to convince him that there wasn't any real evidence of a connection because there *wasn't* a connection. Besides, they were perpetrated by people who understand evidence. These murders weren't committed by some dumb street thugs."

"You're probably right about there not being a tie-in, but since Steve was obsessed by the cases, they might have some bearing on his murder. If you could send me whatever information you can on the cases that he thought were in the group, I'd appreciate it."

Actually, I'd begun to think that Winter might have been right. Proving it was going to be the hard part. On the other hand, I might have been falling down the same rabbit hole.

"Sure. For some of those, I can give you the whole thing since they've been to court and it's all part of the public record. But you aren't going to find anything."

"Thanks, but I'd still like to look at them. One last thing. Did Steve have any suspects in mind for his serial killer?"

"He had a profile. But no one he was willing to name, or maybe no one he was willing to tell me about. It was sad, but when I started to resist his ideas, he pretty much cut me off. I haven't talked to him in almost four years. Did you talk to his ex-wife? I expect she'll be making the arrangements."

I told him we'd spoken to her and that that was my impression.

"I'll give her a call and see if I can be of any help. The whole thing is just sad. Look, I'll send what I can on those cases as soon as I can get it pulled together. Not like I have much else to do. Bad knee and less than six months until I retire. They have me tied to a desk."

I had to wait for my last Texas interview to call me back. After the introductions, Major Melvin Travis told me he was knee-deep in alligators, but he could give me a couple of minutes for ol' Winter. Melvin didn't disappoint with his Texas drawl and deep bourbon-and-cigars voice.

"Hell of thing about Steve. Good man, just didn't know when to let go of the bear. We all tried to tell him. Really hated to see him go. He was an ol' style Texas Ranger, gun and guts. How can I help?"

I told him most of what I'd learned from Sue and Roger. "It would help if you could fill in some of the details from a supervisor's viewpoint."

"Yep, they were all good friends. 'Course, everyone liked Steve. Hard not to. Like I said, we all tried to turn that horse, but he wasn't havin' none of it. Got the bit in his teeth and was running wild. We let him go for a couple of cases like Roger told you. Steve had been right about almost every case he'd ever worked on, but I think being accused of a crime did somethin' to his mind. Messed with it.

"That one case that he screwed up for the prosecution… I had to stick my neck way on out there to save him on that one. Austin wanted him fired over that. But even after that fiasco, he wouldn't stop. One day about three years ago, we had a sit-down with him and explained that this could end one of two ways. Either he was going to start following the directions of his superiors, or he was going to lay his star on the desk. He chose to leave. He had enough time in that we were able to push it through as a retirement. I think even if he hadn't agreed, I would have been able to get him a medical retirement. I think he had PTSD, to tell you the truth. That Linda Reeves case put him through the ringer. Lot of officers would have had problems. Messed up his marriage too."

"I'd like to review the Reeves case and any others that Steve thought might involve the same killer."

"Whoa! You aren't going to try to stir up a bunch of dust, are you?"

"No, of course not. I just want to get an idea of his mindset. See what he saw. Understanding the victim helps me to see who the suspects might be."

"Exactly what I tell the new boys and girls coming in here. Sure, I'll give ol' Roger the greenlight. Guy needs some work anyway. Now, for any active cases, you'll need to come on out here to look at those. We can't let active files leave the building."

I told him I understood and thanked him for all his help.

The million-dollar question was: was Winter crazy? His cases seemed very similar to the Harper and Baxter cases.

CHAPTER NINETEEN

I looked at my watch and it was already past noon. I found Darlene hunched over her computer, typing up a report.

"Wanna catch lunch?"

"I miss Winston's," she sighed, referencing what had previously been the best restaurant in town. It had been closed ever since we arrested the owner for being a batshit crazy serial killer.

"We could try the new taco stand. It's really not that—"

"Sheriff wants to see you guys!" my dad's assistant shouted at us from the door.

"So much for lunch," I said.

Major Parks was in Dad's office when we got there. Mauser came over and greeted us playfully. The more people there were in the room, the more excited he got. I guess he figured it was a party.

"Go lay down," Dad told the dog after he'd bumped into everyone in the room repeatedly, trying to get attention. The odds of Mauser obeying Dad were directly correlated to whether Mauser *wanted* to do as instructed, but today he'd apparently had enough of the meet-and-greet. He surprised me by going over and flopping down on his mattress.

"Sit down," Dad told us in the same tone that he'd just

used with Mauser. "Major Parks has submitted his report on Deputy Henley's behavior at the public softball game. For conduct which reflected poorly on this department, I'm suspending Henley for five days without pay and putting a written reprimand in his file. Since he's already been out for more than five days and since we're shorthanded, I'm willing to simply withhold the five days' pay and let him return to work. However, I want to hear where the investigation into Todd Harper's murder currently stands before I approve his return to duty." Dad rattled this speech off like a judge before a jury.

I looked at Darlene, wondering which of us should answer. I thought it would sound better coming from her since she would come across as less biased. She saw my look and understood.

"Macklin and I have been comparing the murders here with a series of others in Texas. I don't want to jump to any conclusions, but I think we can say that there is a very real chance that the murders are linked, which would eliminate Henley as a suspect."

"That sounds good, but can you give me some details?" I knew that Dad wanted Pete back, but he needed to be hardnosed for the sake of the department.

"The murder which appears to have set all of this in motion occurred fifteen years ago ..." I started, giving the broad outlines of the Linda Reeves case and emphasizing the similarities between it and the Harper case—softball, an accused law enforcement officer and a baseball bat used as the murder weapon. I let Darlene flesh it out with some additional information that she had gathered that morning. Finally, we left them with the image of a murderer who seemed to be pulling the strings from behind a curtain.

Dad looked back and forth between Darlene and me. "That's a complicated explanation for a murder that would appear to be a simple case of a mad dad with a baseball bat," he said.

"Occam's razor," I said. "Our killer employs it like a

secret weapon to obscure what has really happened. That's what sank poor Steve Winter. He was faced with trying to convince people that the complicated answer was the correct one."

We also used the reports from Landon to buttress our argument. Having an outside source would give Dad some cover if things went south.

Major Parks was staring at us as though we'd lost our minds. Dad, however, seemed intrigued by the idea of a multi-state serial killer. At least, he liked it more than having one of his own deputies as a suspect. As for Maxwell, as much as Dad would have liked to throw him under the bus, he didn't believe that the man had killed his cantankerous old neighbor.

"I don't know if I can buy all of what you're selling, but I'm comfortable letting Pete come back," he said as I worked hard not to think of the end of the bat sitting in my safe deposit box. How would Dad feel if he knew about that?

He grilled us a little more about the state of the investigation, made a few suggestions and promised to poke the folks at the state lab to expedite the tests.

As we were walking out the door, Darlene hit her arm against the wall hard enough make a pretty good *thud*.

"Damn it! That's the second time today that I've banged my knuckles. Now I've got to worry about when the third time is going to come along."

"Yep, trouble comes in threes," Parks agreed as he followed us out the door.

Threes? I thought. Something about that bothered me. What about threes? We had three murders. So that was three. We had Winter and Reeves. That was two. Two people that were involving themselves in the murder of Todd Harper. Was there a third?

I was so lost in thought that I almost bumped into Darlene when she stopped at the front door.

"You still want to go get lunch?" she asked.

I looked at my watch, which now told me it was two-thirty. "More like linner… or maybe diunch," I said.

"I like linner," Darlene laughed.

"Sure, I'm in."

When I got in the car, Darlene turned to me.

"What's on your mind?"

"Your hand. Threes."

"What?"

"I don't know. I think I've got the tail end of something. Let's go get our linner. Maybe it will come to me."

Halfway through my second soft taco, I knew what had been bugging me.

"I've got our third."

"Third what?"

"We've had two people sticking their noses into the Harper case. First Winter and then Reeves. But there is a third."

"There's the killer. He's certainly involved."

My phone buzzed with a text from Pete that read: *I'm baaaaaaack!*

"Dad told Pete he's reinstated," I said.

"Forget about your bromance for a minute. What are you talking about?"

"Who's the third person who's been nosing around this case? Who's been wanting to look at reports?"

"Oh," Darlene said as it dawned on her. "But we went to him. Sort of." I could see the wheels turning in her head.

"Tell me exactly, how did Landon's involvement come about? Did you approach him first or did he approach you?"

"Kind of both. I saw him at a meeting of the Friends of the Library. But now that you mention it, he approached me, though he made it seem like it was just one of those things that happens. Looking back, he initiated the conversation, but that could mean he was only being friendly or was looking for some consulting work."

"Granted, he might just be good at networking. Then again, maybe he's really good at manipulating people."

"Which is a quality we've assigned to our killer."

"Correct." I stuffed the rest of my taco in my mouth and wiped my lips. I could tell that Darlene had lost her appetite as she stared off into the distance, lost in thought.

"Let's go," she said, wrapping up her half-eaten burrito and putting it back into the bag. As she stood up, her napkin fell on the ground between the table and the bench. When she reached down for it, she cracked her knuckle on the wood. "Ouch! Knew the third was coming."

On the way back to the office, we decided that each of us would take a part of Landon's personal history and see if there were any holes in it or ties to Texas.

I dug up the CV he'd given us and we split up his references. He'd graduated from high school in Missouri and went to college in Ohio. His first degree was in criminology. He had worked as a tech with a couple of police departments to pay for college. Eventually, he ended up with a masters in criminology and a doctorate in psychology. He had taught at three universities in the last twenty years, one in Alabama, one in Louisiana and finally the University of Central Florida.

Darlene agreed to take his early years up through college while I followed up on the three university jobs. By the time we'd parceled everything out, it was after five.

"No point trying to get anyone now," I said.

"Agreed." Darlene looked frustrated. "But I hate stopping now. I want to develop at least one good suspect. I hate feeling like we're just shooting in the dark."

Cara didn't come over that evening as she had early-morning duties at the vet. I thought about mentioning that staying at her place when it was more convenient for her job wouldn't be an option if she moved in with me on a permanent basis, but I decided I wouldn't kick that alligator.

That night I texted back and forth with Pete, who was happy to be coming back to work, but frustrated that he was still banned from working on the Harper murder. We decided that we'd try to get Dad and Lt. Johnson to fudge the point by letting him work on the Baxter and Winter cases. After involving Darlene in the text-a-thon, she'd agreed to join us in arguing for Pete's help. He couldn't be in on the general discussions of the cases, as those would no doubt cover all three murders, but Darlene and I would be able to give Pete specific assignments related to the Baxter or Winter murders.

On Thursday I hit the phone running, calling all three universities that Landon had listed on his CV. They all checked out, leaving me to wonder if my paranoia was running wild. Still, I couldn't get it out of my head that there was something odd about the way Landon had insinuated himself into the case. But I couldn't get around the fact that, ultimately, we'd asked for his help.

I was mulling all of this over in my head when my phone rang. Speak of the devil.

"I was wondering if you had the preliminary autopsy report on Winter yet," he asked.

I was looking at my email where the report from Dr. Darzi was fourth from the top in my inbox. But I still hadn't talked to Darlene about her research into Landon's background, so I didn't feel like we had cleared him.

"No, not yet," I said, deciding that I'd just lie about the report. I really didn't want to give it to him yet, but didn't have any good reason to completely cut him off from the investigation.

"I was heading that way so I just thought I'd give you a call," he continued, then hesitated. "I also wouldn't mind looking over the evidence that you collected at the scene of Winter's murder. I'm working at integrating that into the profile of the murderer from the first two attacks. I figured I would do four profiles, one for the killer in each of the murders and then a profile that assumes that the killer is the same in each case. That will allow us to do a compare-and-contrast between the different profiles."

It all sounded good, but he was pushing. Or at least that was the impression I was getting. I didn't like it.

"That sounds great. Look, we'll give you a call when we get the autopsy report and maybe then we'll have the final reports from the other cases." I was pretty determined at this point to put him off.

"I just thought that since I was going to be near the office, I'd come by and look at the evidence. I might be able to help you evaluate what you've collected. Save you time in the long run and give me a head start on my reports."

Pushing way too hard. Now he was irritating me. "Like I said, we'll give you a call," I said, more harshly than I intended, but I was through with the conversation and he didn't seem willing to take no for an answer.

There was a long silence on his end of the call. I knew that he'd picked up on my tone. It would have been hard not to. "Okay. I'll wait to hear from you," he said coldly and disconnected.

What the hell, I thought. *Why should I care if he's mad?*

I found Darlene at her desk, finishing up a phone call. After she hung up, I filled her in on my conversation with Landon.

"Yeah, apparently he's always been a bit pushy," she said. "I tracked down his advisor from college when he was working on his criminology degree. The lady said that he was obsessed with going into law enforcement. He apparently made it through the academy and joined a local department in Ohio, but didn't make it through the probation period. I called the department, but they didn't have his records on file anymore so they couldn't tell me why he was washed out. They promised to try and find someone who might remember him being there."

"So?" I asked.

"I don't know. Without a connection to Texas, what do we have? You know, he could just be a jerk."

"True."

"A jerk, a wannabe and someone who's looking for consultant money. Adds up to pushy," Darlene said. She had a point, but that would land us right back where we were, without a good suspect. Being stubborn and still put out by his attitude on the phone, I said that I wanted to look into him a bit more.

Walking back to my desk, I saw Pete come in. He was all smiles with his gold star hooked on his belt and his gun on his hip.

"Good to see you."

"Damn right," he said with a grin, shaking my hand. "Give me something to work on. I want to nab the son of a bitch who tried to frame me."

I told him what Darlene and I had been doing all morning.

"You really think he could be a suspect?"

"I did. But going over his CV, I'm not seeing any holes. And if we can't place him in Texas, then we can't connect him to any of the murders there."

"And you went over all his references?"

I picked up Landon's CV and looked at it again. "I went over all the references that he gave me on this piece of paper that he prepared with the references that he wanted us to see," I said with a full measure of irony, realizing the possibly huge assumption that I'd made. I turned to my computer and did a quick search for Landon. I vaguely remembered seeing a LinkedIn page come up when I had searched before. I found it and took a look at the employment history listed there.

The Louisiana university that he showed on his CV wasn't listed. Instead, the LinkedIn page seemed to just blur over that period of time by stretching the employment dates from his previous position to meet up with the one that the CV said came after Louisiana.

Pete was following along over my shoulder. I pulled up the Louisiana university's website. All of the contact numbers for the university started with the same three-number prefix. The prefix on the contact number listed on the CV was different.

"That isn't a number for the university," I said, pointing

to the CV.

"Think he came up with a false reference to cover a period of time he didn't want you to know about?" Pete suggested.

I called the human resources office listed on the Louisiana university's website. Ten minutes later, I'd been assured that no one by the name of Edward Landon had ever worked there.

Next, I called the number on the CV and the same sweet-sounding lady that I'd spoken to earlier that morning answered. "Human Resources, may I help you?"

"Yes, hi, we talked earlier. I'm Deputy Macklin from the Adams County Sheriff's Office."

"Oh, yes, I remember. But we're pretty busy here at the moment. How can I help you?"

"I just wanted to double-check. Doctor Landon worked there for five years, is that right?"

"Let me look at his record again. Like I said, we're very busy here in the office." I was put on hold for several minutes. "Yes, that is correct," she finally responded, reading off the years and the different positions he'd held, including full professor.

"Listen to me. I know that you aren't working for the university. I'm leading a criminal investigation into a case that involves multiple homicides." Before I could say anything else, the phone went dead.

I sent her a text: *If you don't call me right back, I will hunt you down and throw your ass in jail.*

In less than five minutes, my phone rang. The number was for the woman on the CV, but when I answered, there was only silence.

"You need to talk to me," I said.

Finally she spoke. "How do I know you are a cop?"

"If you want, you can Google the Adams County Sheriff's Office in Florida, call them and have them patch you through to me."

"No. I believe you. I knew this was too good."

"What was too good?"

"A craigslist ad. It said I could make easy money. This guy sent me a phone and all I had to do was keep it with me. He gave me a script to read if anyone called and asked about him. When I told him I was laid up with a bad back and couldn't go anywhere, he said that was perfect. He paid me a thousand dollars and said that I'd get a hundred for every call and a thousand a month, calls or no calls."

"When did you answer the ad?"

"A month ago."

"Did you ever meet the guy?"

"No. We emailed and then talked on the phone a couple of times," she said and then added, "Oh, yeah, and I text him whenever someone calls." This sent a shiver running down my spine.

"Did you text him today."

"Yeah," she said reluctantly, knowing I wouldn't be happy.

I got her name, address, another phone number and email before assuring her that, right now, she was only a witness and that, as long as she cooperated from this point forward, we wouldn't press charges. She asked about the money and I told her that she would probably be able to keep what she had and might even be able to sue Landon for more. I figured dangling a carrot like that couldn't hurt to ensure her cooperation.

Once I was off the phone, Darlene, Pete and I went into the conference room to discuss how we should proceed.

"Top of the list," I said in answer to Darlene's question of where this left Landon.

"One word of caution," Darlene said. "I hate to be the wet blanket, but we still need to keep our eyes open for other possibilities. If we get tunnel vision, we might miss another suspect, or we might screw up the prosecution of Landon if he *is* the murderer," Darlene said.

Pete and I nodded in agreement. Each of us knew of cases where the defense had hammered the prosecution because law enforcement had focused on the defendant and never considered other suspects.

"What we know now is that Landon has lied about his résumé," I said. "Specifically, it appears that he lied to us. And spent a bit of time and money to make us believe the lie."

"People lie about their résumés all the time," Darlene said, playing devil's advocate.

"True," Pete said. "But this lie covered the time of the murders in Texas. The murders that had Winter all worked up." I'd filled Pete in on Winter's history and timeline.

"We know what type of work Landon did," I said. "We know the time frame. It should be a simple matter to contact all of the colleges and universities within a hundred mile radius of the Texas murders and see if they employed an Edward Landon."

As we were talking, my phone was sitting on the table in front of me. I'd turned the ringer off while I was making calls that morning and it started vibrating now. I looked at it, saw that it was Dad, and decided to ignore it while we continued our conversation.

"It's your dad. Maybe you should answer it," Darlene said. She was sitting across the table and had read the caller ID.

Instead of answering the phone, I just stared at her. I looked down at the phone, which vibrated for another minute before going to voicemail, then back at Darlene.

"What?" Darlene asked as I continued to stare at her. "Is there something stuck in my teeth?"

Something was digging its way up from the dark recesses of my mind. I didn't want to do anything that might scare it away.

"If you're having a stroke, blink twice," Darlene said, beginning to sound annoyed.

"The trigger," I finally said.

"What trigger?" Pete asked, no doubt thinking I was talking about a gun.

"The trigger event that got Winter killed."

Darlene wasn't looking irritated anymore and she leaned forward attentively.

"I couldn't get it out of my head that some event must have caused our killer to decide to murder Winter when he did. According to our theory, they'd been playing a cat-and-mouse game for years. But why, all of a sudden, did the mouse decide that the cat had to go? Let's assume that Landon is the killer. Winter has chased him for years, and Landon played along. But then Landon moved here. He set up a false résumé, trying to leave his past behind him. Why? Possibly to go on another killing spree. To do that, he needed to have room to operate without Winter looking over his shoulder."

"I can buy that," Darlene said, "assuming, of course, that he is the killer."

"Right. Now he's killed twice. He's in control, has the local sheriff's office on the end of his string. He's playing us along, having a good old time. What happens when he's sitting in here talking with us?"

Darlene squinted her eyes in concentration. "Did your phone go off?"

"Exactly. Winter called me. I'd put his name in my contacts so that, when it rang, Landon was able to see who was calling me from across the table just as you did when my dad called."

"Son of a—"

"He realizes that Winter's in town and that he's already talked to us."

"So he needed to get him out of the way, fast," Pete said.

"I'll buy that," Darlene said. "So we need to nail down that connection with Texas."

We went back to Darlene's desk, where she did a quick Google search that came up with a dozen colleges and universities within a hundred miles of where Linda Reeves was murdered. We split the list up between us. Less than an hour later, Pete shouted, "Bingo!" He'd found a college less than twenty miles from the crime that confirmed Landon had taught there.

"We need to get a warrant for his house," Darlene said. "I'm going to see Shantel and go over the evidence that we've collected so far. I'll see if any of it looks promising in light of our new suspect."

"We can go back over the CCTV footage too. Now that we know who and what kind of car we're looking for." I was excited now, glad to have a solid suspect.

Darlene headed back to the evidence room while Pete and I decided how we wanted to proceed. Pete's phone buzzed with a text message and he casually took it out of his pocket and glanced at it. He texted regularly with his wife and daughters, so Pete getting a text was business as usual. I didn't pay any attention until he jumped up and started running for the door.

CHAPTER TWENTY

Pete never ran. At his size, if he ran it was a newsworthy event. For a moment I stood in shock, watching him charge past the desks toward the door. Then I came to my senses and ran after him, yelling his name.

He almost knocked down another deputy who was coming through the front door. The stunned man called out, "Hey, Pete, what's up?" but Pete never heard him. I just shrugged as I ran past him, still calling for Pete.

I finally caught up with him as he charged into the parking lot. When I grabbed his arm, he turned on me and, for a second, I thought he was going to slug me.

"Let go of me!" he said menacingly.

"Tell me what this is about!"

He let loose with a string of four-letter words that I had never heard him use and ended with, "Let go of me, now!" His face was a bright red, his eyes small black pinpoints.

"No. Tell me what's going on and then I'll let you go," I said, knowing that I was risking a punch from his melon-sized fists.

Instead of clobbering me, he jerked his phone out of his pocket and fumbled across the screen with shaking hands before turning it to show me a text message. It simply said:

Come to my house alone—Ed. I felt my bowels loosen when I saw the image that accompanied the text. Kim was sitting in the passenger seat of a car, slumped down with her hands tied and tape over her mouth.

It took a minute for my mind to process the situation. My hand dropped from Pete's arm and he turned, hurrying for his car. I knew what I had to do. Almost before Pete was behind the steering wheel, I was in the passenger seat beside him.

"Listen to me. We can't be stupid. We can't rush into this without assessing the situation," I said as he started the car.

He didn't say a word as he backed up and hit the car behind us before slamming into drive and tearing out of the parking lot.

Pete drove like a man possessed, the car's siren screaming. I tried to reason with him as we both ignored the dispatch radio that was squawking for our attention. Pete didn't say a word the entire time. I'm not even sure that he heard me or the radio until we were within a couple of miles of Landon's house. Then Pete flipped the siren off, gradually slowing the car down.

An eighth of a mile from the driveway, Pete pulled over. Breathing heavily, he turned to me and growled, "Talk."

I'd been working on a plan, searching my mind to remember the layout of Landon's house.

"Okay, first of all, he knows that we're coming. So whatever plan we come up with has to take that into consideration."

"Let me be clear. I only have one goal and that's to save Kim. Nothing else matters. Nothing. Talk faster."

"We aren't going to be able to save her if we get killed before we find her. Agreed?"

"I'm listening."

"The man knows law enforcement. He's been manipulating us from the start. This is just another attempt to do that. Front door is out. Back door is almost certainly out too." Even as I said this, I realized that we may not have

205

had any other options.

"There's only one of him."

"He could have booby traps."

"Enough. Let's go!"

Pete threw open the door and got out while I failed to come up with any other viable option. I joined him at the trunk of the car, where he pulled out a Mossberg 500 shotgun and started loading it with shells. He grabbed a mix of slugs and buckshot, loading as many as the magazine would take. I grabbed the two body armor vests and handed the larger one to him. Luckily, we all kept an extra one in our trunks in case we ever needed to protect a victim at a crime scene. I hurriedly put mine on and was relieved to see Pete taking the time to fully strap his on. He took an extra magazine out of his range bag for his Glock 21 handgun and I found a couple extra ones for my 17. All of this seemed like overkill for one middle-aged retired professor, but I wouldn't bet my life on it.

Pete started off down the road like a bear charging a dumpster. I didn't have too hard of a time keeping up.

"At least let's take the time to go around the house. One time, just to get the lay of the land. Maybe we'll see a better way in," I reasoned.

Pete slowed down as we got close to the driveway. I grabbed his arm.

"He could have a camera or sensors on the road. Let's cut through the woods."

Pete just nodded and crossed the ditch to the line of field fencing that marked Landon's property. The fence was four feet high and, looking at it, I wasn't sure how he was going to get over it. I needn't have worried. When Pete got to the fence, he just threw his body against the wire. Staples popped out of the posts as his three hundred pounds pushed the fence to the ground. He lumbered over it and I followed close behind.

We certainly weren't quiet as we crunched through the underbrush, but at least we weren't heading straight up

Landon's driveway. It probably took us an extra five minutes to come within sight of the house. Everything appeared quiet and perfectly normal from the outside.

Walking slower now, we circled the house, staying behind cover as much as possible. I didn't fool myself into thinking that we were sneaking up on him. I was pretty sure that he knew we were outside by now. I just hoped that we could find a way in that didn't involve the blatantly obvious. As we reached the far side of the house, I comforted myself with the thought that at least we hadn't been shot at yet.

Landon could only have had a few motives for sending that image. The best bet was that he wanted Pete to come charging in and get himself killed. The second option was that this was all a misdirection, and he was currently on his way out of the state with Kim as a hostage. The last option was unthinkable—that he wanted Pete to find him after he'd killed Kim, either so he could commit suicide by cop, or so that he could kill Pete after having tortured him with the sight of his daughter's body. I shook off that gruesome thought and focused on the house.

All of the windows were more than six feet off of the ground. My impression of the house after going around it was that the thing was built like a nineteenth-century brick fort. The only practical ways in were the front or back doors.

Pete turned to me. "You don't have to do this."

"Forget it. I'm coming with you."

"Okay, then. Front door or back door?"

"Whoever has the shotgun should take the front door. They'll need it to breach the lock."

"Agreed. There's already a slug in the chamber. Which do you want?"

"Front door," I said and Pete solemnly handed me the Mossberg and the shells he'd stuffed in his pocket.

"When I hear you fire, I'll go in through the back door."

"I'm not going to hesitate. Once I'm out in the open, I'm going for the door."

"I'll be ready," he said and put his hand on my shoulder.

"Thanks."

"Good luck."

As I started out into the open, I apologized to God for not talking to him more often and asked him to take care of Kim and Pete. I jogged into the front yard, then ran toward the brick steps leading onto the porch. I took the steps two at a time, counting on my rubber-soled shoes not to slip. I never hesitated, but went straight to the door and rammed the shotgun against the fancy electronic door lock. I pulled the trigger and the gun rammed back against my shoulder as the slug smashed its way through the door, sending wood, metal and plastic flying.

I kicked the door in and heard a second shotgun blast. I caught some of the flash and was half-blinded. I turned and fired a round to the left of the door where the shot had come from. No one shot back and, as my eyesight returned, I saw what was left of a jerry-rigged booby trap using an engraved over-and-under shotgun.

Trying not to think how close that had been, I turned to face the hall and saw someone running toward me. It was Pete, gun in hand and heading for the staircase. It took me a second to realize that he was chasing someone, then I heard footsteps on the stairs above us.

Pete was already pounding up the stairs when I smelled something burning and saw smoke coming from the back of the house. I knew that the house was on fire, but it didn't matter. I followed Pete up the stairs. The big guy was laboring as he went up and I caught up with him at the first landing. I tried to look up, hoping not to see someone pointing a gun down at us.

We reached the second floor where we were faced with the choice of four doors. More and more smoke was drifting up from below and I could hear smoke detectors going off throughout the house.

"I saw him," Pete said, gasping to catch his breath. "He tried to douse me with gasoline. I got a shot off, but missed him."

"We've got to hurry."

I turned to the nearest door and kicked it open. I cleared the room and heard Pete smash in another door across the hall. We came out of the rooms at almost the same time and bashed into the last two doors almost simultaneously. As soon as I was sure that no one was in mine, I rushed over to the room where Pete had gone. He came out alone, confused and panicked. Then I saw his eyes open wide and he started firing back toward the staircase. I turned to see a ladder extending down from the attic and Landon dodging the shots as Pete fired.

Landon also had a gun, but when one of Pete's shots hit him square in the body armor he was wearing, he dropped it. We rushed over to him and Pete dropped down on top of Landon. I just caught sight of the flash of steel as Landon went to thrust a knife into Pete's side. Without thinking, I let my body go and fell down onto Landon's arm.

I felt a searing pain in my side. He'd managed to slip the blade into the opening between the front and back of my vest. He pulled it out quickly, no doubt planning to stab me again, but dropped it as Pete pummeled his side with his fists. At last, Landon went limp. The smoke was almost too thick to see through now and I thought I could hear the flames getting closer.

Where is Kim? my mind screamed. Then I realized that I wasn't just hearing the question in my own mind. Pete was yelling it over and over into Landon's face, but Landon wasn't saying a word.

"We have to get out of here!" I shouted to Pete, but I knew he'd never leave until he was sure that Kim wasn't in the house.

"Look for her!" he yelled to me and then went back to working on Landon, who was beginning to smile.

I clambered awkwardly up the ladder to the attic, the shotgun now slung over my shoulder. At the top of the ladder I found only darkness. I pulled out my small Maglite and did a once-over of the area, calling Kim's name. There was nothing up there but insulation and a few packing boxes. I could barely breathe now as the smoke rose to fill the space. I went back down the ladder, half sliding to the bottom.

"She's not here!"

Landon was now bloody and handcuffed, but still defiant. With a huge growl, Pete grabbed Landon by his collar and dragged him down the stairs. By the time we coughed and gagged our way to the ground floor, the flames were coming down the hallway toward the front door. To my surprise, Pete turned toward the advancing fire rather than the safety of the front door.

I saw him lift Landon and then, in a feat of strength that I can only credit to adrenaline and desperation, he held the monster over the flames. The fire leaped up, tasting Landon's legs, and, for the first time, he looked well and truly scared. He held out longer than seemed possible, but finally screamed, "She escaped! I swear to you, she escaped!"

The legs of his pants were on fire now and I tugged on Pete, who seemed surprised that he'd gotten an answer. With Landon now screaming in panic, Pete snapped out of it and we all ran for the front door. Outside, Pete unceremoniously dropped Landon on the ground and rolled him about until the fire was out.

I took several deep breaths of fresh air, then I pulled out my phone and called dispatch, asking them to send backup and a fire engine. Then I went over to Pete, who held out the keys to his car.

"Get the car. He says that she stabbed him in the leg with a pen and escaped from his car about five miles away."

I looked down and, sure enough, there was a bloody hole in Landon's pants. I took the keys and jogged down the driveway. I could feel that my shirt and pants were damp with blood, but adrenaline was masking the pain.

When I got back with the car, Pete tossed Landon in the backseat and switched places with me, ramming the car into gear and speeding down the driveway. Landon whined loudly about needing medical attention, but we ignored him.

"I told her, if she was ever walking along a road alone, to move into the bushes if a car was coming."

At the five-mile point, Pete slowed the car, moving at a pace that would allow someone looking out from the bushes to see who was driving. Pete honked the horn every couple of minutes. We tried to get Landon to give us more details about where Kim had escaped, but he'd gone back to stonewalling us.

"Would she know which way town was?" I asked Pete.

"I think so. We take this road out to the lake to fish several times during the summer."

I was about to suggest that we turn around when I saw a flash of white out of the corner of my eye. Kim was running out of the woods toward the car. Pete must have seen her at the same moment, as he slammed on the brakes and sent Landon crashing into the back of my seat.

Pete leaped out of the car and ran to his daughter. I got out in time to see the two of them embrace. I was feeling light-headed. *Must be all the smoke*, I thought, watching Pete and Kim hug each other with huge grins on their faces and tears running down their cheeks. I could hear sirens approaching in the distance.

Pete wrapped his arm around his daughter and they started walking back to the car. Pete's smile faltered, replaced by concern as he looked at me, then the world went black.

CHAPTER TWENTY-ONE

I awoke in the early hours of Friday morning, my ears ringing with the incessant beeping of a heart monitor and the sounds of all the other equipment that hospital staff use to make sure their patients are still alive. I was immediately aware of two things—a dull, throbbing pain that seemed to fill my entire left side and a warm, comforting grip on my right hand. I turned my head to see Cara sitting beside me, unaware that I was awake. Her eyes were red and rimmed with shadows.

I squeezed her hand weakly and whispered, "Hey, you."

Her head snapped toward me and the pain receded for a moment under the power of her fierce smile. She leaped from her chair and bent over me, resting her forehead against mine and kissing me gently.

"Larry, you dumbass, you scared the hell out of us!" she said through happy tears.

Us? That's when I realized we weren't alone.

My dad sat in a chair on the other side of my bed, his uniform shirt wrinkled and half unbuttoned and his hair a mess. He looked at me and started to say, "Son, I'm—" *Is he choking up?* I wondered. Then he stood quickly and left the ICU cubicle.

Baffled, I looked at Cara.

"He hasn't left your side for a second," she said. "He was afraid he'd lose you like he lost your mom. He really does love you almost as much as Mauser, you know."

As usual, he has a damn funny way of showing it, I thought. But I was too tired and in too much pain to say anything. I just smiled at Cara and drifted off again.

A few hours later, having been thoroughly poked and prodded by a team of nurses and doctors, I found out just how lucky I'd been. The knife had gone deep into my side, but while the surgeons had been able to repair the internal damage, they'd had a hard time stopping all the bleeding. It had taken one blood transfusion, more than two hours of surgery and an impressive collection of stitches to patch me up, making the first twelve hours touch-and-go for me and full of worry for Cara and my dad.

Dad never mentioned his abrupt departure from my room, probably hoping I'd been barely conscious and hadn't noticed. But Cara told me how she'd found him later, alone in a family waiting room and quietly sobbing. The old man kept most of his feelings bottled up—except anger; he was good at expressing anger—but I had always suspected that the rough waters ran deep. Cara told me that she'd simply held him until his tears had dried. I figured it was probably good for him.

The doctors and nurses came and went several times that day, each time looking more and more as if they were bored with me. One of the doctors even made a point of telling me that the only reason I was in ICU was because of the amount of blood I'd lost. He seemed to imply that any normal person would have had enough sense to get to the hospital faster, which would have saved them all a lot of time and trouble.

The next morning, I was finally released to a regular room. That's when I was able to see the other person who'd been keeping a near-continuous vigil.

Pete had come to the hospital as soon as he was done processing Landon and had seen Kim safely home. He'd been pacing the halls outside of the ICU the entire time, frustrated at the family-only policy that the hospital had instated for me—with an exception made for Cara at my dad's insistence. Pete had refused to leave until Cara was finally was able to assure him that I was awake and would survive another day to aid and abet him in taking more stupid chances.

Now he walked slowly into my room, his hands in his pockets and his expression equal parts relieved, sheepish and grateful.

Eager to deflect attention away from myself, I quickly asked, "How's Kim?"

"Great. She's great. Been bragging to everyone about her escape. After we got you in the ambulance, she insisted on riding with me to the jail to book Landon. The whole way there, she lectured him about what she thought of his evil ways. I was even able to take her back with us to help fingerprint him. He was humiliated to be booked in by a teenage girl.

"I won't have to worry about her having nightmares about her abduction. Instead she's going to have honest-to-God dreams about it. She's more determined than ever to go into law enforcement. And then there's you, you stupid idiot. I didn't know he'd stabbed you."

"You were a little preoccupied."

Pete's gaze fell on several flower arrangements that had been waiting in the room for me. I hadn't even had a chance to read the cards yet. His eyes widened at one vase in particular. "You aren't going to believe who these are from," he said, taking the card and handing it to me.

The card read:

Roses are red,
Violets are blue,
Even an idiot can find a clue.

214

Thanks for solving this one,
  Maxwell.
P.S.—Maybe I won't fire your ass after I beat your dad this fall.

"What a nice sentiment," I muttered.

Pete pulled a flash drive out of his pocket. "Let's see if this works. It'll cheer you up," he said, plugging it into a USB port on the TV.

"If this is a porn film, I'd rather not."

"This is law enforcement porn," Pete said. "I thought you might want to see the interview we did with Landon yesterday afternoon." He pushed a couple of buttons on the remote and managed to pull up the video.

High-quality cameras were installed in our interview rooms, so the picture was good. The angle was odd since the cameras were mounted high on the walls, but Landon's arrogance still came shining through.

Pete and Darlene sat on one side of the table, with Landon shackled to the other side. Lt. Johnson stood by the door. I didn't see Dad, but assumed that he had been watching from a monitor in his office. I knew he wouldn't have wanted to miss this one.

Pete fast-forwarded through the preliminaries.

"I guess I'm in trouble no matter what. Texas is as likely to put me in the chair as Florida," Landon stated.

"We aren't going to make any deals with you," Johnson said. "If you think that's what this is about, then we may as well close down shop now." Johnson was too much of a straight shooter to make a good interrogator. I'm sure Landon knew he was screwed and was glad for the opportunity to play for the cameras.

As if hearing my thoughts, he looked up directly into the lens. "No. I'm good. Ask your questions."

"Why did you target Todd Harper?" Darlene asked.

"Because of this dumbass deputy. I was looking for some fun and when I saw that video go up, I thought, 'Here we go.' And I absolutely loved the similarity to Linda Reeves's murder. Of course, now that I think about it, that may have been a mistake. Kind of like sending up a flare for good old Steve Winter…"

"How did you set up the murder so fast if you didn't know the victim before seeing the video that night?" Darlene asked.

"Are you kidding? Where have you been hiding? I just read the comments that went with the video and learned almost everything I needed to know. And it's not like a baseball bat is hard to come by."

"But how did you know where he lived? His name wasn't even on the lease."

"I already told you. From the comments, I was able to draw out who his friends were and who he was living with. I went to his place, scoped it out and got lucky. He was the last person to go to bed. All I had to do was come up behind the stupid, intoxicated lout and bash him in the head."

"Where is the weapon you used in the assault?" Darlene asked, and I could see Pete squirming on film.

"Funny about that. I snuck into this guy's backyard and put the charred remains in his grill. I guess that never got reported. How strange."

Everyone looked at Pete.

"I clean out my grill by dumping the ashes in my burn barrel. If it was in there, I must have missed it," Pete responded, and everyone seemed to study him for a moment. I heard Darlene clear her throat.

"Deputy Henley, I'd suggest that we look at your burn barrel. Not that we need that weapon at this point," Johnson said.

"Let me stop you there," Landon said. "This gets to my motive. You might wonder why I've chosen to screw with law enforcement officers. This is why." He tried to wave his hands, but the shackles limited his movement. "Cops. Always thinking they're something special. My field training officer refused to sign off on me, but I can promise you I was the smartest guy in that room…"

Pete keyed the remote again. "You can listen to him talk

about himself some other time. I heard enough of it as it was." He hit play again.

"Who set the meeting up in our parking lot? You or Winter?"

"Oh, that was me all the way. First thing I did when I came to town was check out the security here at the department. I'd been thinking all along about leaving you a surprise in the parking lot. I just got lucky the way it worked out with Steve. He was so arrogant. It was easy. I told him I wanted to meet and suggested the sheriff's office. I don't think it ever crossed his mind that I would kill him.

"While we were having a little chat, he told me that he thought I was too big of chicken to attack a man face to face. He thought I framed cops because I was too scared to attack them directly. Truth is, killing you all would be too easy. It's much more fun to set you up and watch you scurry around with half of you trying to put the other half in jail. You should have seen the expression on his face when I drove the knife into his heart."

We watched an hour more before Pete stopped it.

"Some Texas Rangers are coming in next week to interview him about their cases. They've got a couple of people in jail out there who are probably innocent."

"I take it that Winter's phone and laptop didn't show up in the search of Landon's car or what's left of his house?"

Pete smiled grimly. "No. We got lucky there. I think Landon destroyed them without ever looking at them, figuring they were full of evidence against him."

After Pete left, I texted Sue, the woman who'd worked with Steve in Texas. She'd probably already heard, but I wanted to follow through on my promise to let her know when we had his killer in jail.

The afternoon passed in a blur of visitors, including Darlene, Shantel and Marcus, Julio Ortiz and half a dozen other deputies. Dad and Genie came by late that evening. Any concerns he'd had about my wellbeing had already been replaced with practical matters. He spent a full fifteen minutes grousing about how, with my two trips to the hospital within three months, I was single-handedly screwing up the department's insurance budget. Cara, sitting beside me, had a hard time hiding her smile.

A doctor came to my room first thing on Sunday morning. He gave me a prescription for pain medication, instructions to rest at home for at least a week, and an appointment date to have my stitches checked, then told me that he was kicking me out. I called Cara with the good news.

"I'll be there shortly," she told me.

As eager as they were to get rid of me, hospital policy still required that I leave the premises in a wheelchair. Cara offered to push. As we rode the elevator down to the parking garage, she leaned over my shoulder and whispered in my ear. "I got that stupid envelope from Darlene. We can take care of the... item once you're home." And at that moment I realized just how special Cara really was.

I waited while she brought the car around. As she came over to help me into the car, I grabbed her hand and stopped her.

"I've been thinking," I started, wondering whether it was the near-death experience or the pain meds affecting my judgment. "I've decided I want Alvin to move in with me. Of course, you can come too, if you want."

The look on her face warmed my heart. Cara threw her arms around me in a big hug, sending shockwaves of pain through my body. I groaned. "Whoa, girl, you're killing me!"

"Sorry!" she said, laughing as she apologized. I started to laugh along with her, which caused me even more pain.

"Stop it! I can't take any more." I caught my breath, and she gently came in and gave me a lingering kiss. When she pulled back, I smiled at her and said, "Take us home."

Larry Macklin returns in:

May's Danger
A Larry Macklin Mystery–Book 7

Here's a preview:

My phone rang as I was getting out of the shower. Hearing "The Longest Time," I knew immediately that it was my girlfriend, Cara Laursen. I groaned as I hastily grabbed a towel. If she was calling me this soon after leaving for work, then it could only mean that her car had broken down, she'd forgotten her purse or something else equally inconvenient. The real reason for her call never crossed my mind.

I hurried into the bedroom, still dripping wet and almost falling as I tripped over two boxes of clothes Cara had yet to unpack. Alvin, her Pug, and my tabby cat, Ivy, watched from their perch on the bed, no doubt amused by the creative string of curse words I was uttering. I managed to grab the phone off of the nightstand just before the call went to voicemail.

"Larry, there's a dead body in the clinic."

Standing in my bedroom, mostly naked and still not fully awake, I wasn't prepared to hear those words from Cara. My mind struggled to make sense of what she was saying, but before I could ask any questions, my phone started making more noise. Holding it out, I saw that I had an incoming call from the sheriff's office. Oddly, seeing that number helped to clarify things.

"You called 911?"

"Yes," Cara said, and now I could hear the shock in her quivering voice.

"I'm getting a call from dispatch now. Are you outside? Somewhere safe?"

"I'm in my car. They wanted me to stay on the line, but I

told them I was going to call you."

I was fumbling around, trying to put on my underwear while I talked with her. "I still need to get dressed. It'll be about half an hour before I can get there," I said, searching for my pants. "Look, I've got to hang up, but I'm on my way." I could hear sirens over the phone. "Can you see a patrol car?"

"Yes, they're almost here."

"I'll be there as soon as I can. Love you."

I took the call from dispatch and explained that I already knew and was on the way.

When I pulled up to the curb outside of Dr. Barnhill's veterinary clinic, I was pleased to see that the responding deputies had already cordoned off the area as a crime scene. Cara was sitting sideways in her car in the parking lot, talking with Deputy Julio Ortiz, one of the most dependable guys in the department. I went straight over to them.

"Have you been inside?" I asked Julio as I walked up.

"Definitely dead, lying in the hallway between two of the exam rooms. I took pictures as I went. Our crime scene techs and the coroner's team are on the way."

"Good job. Why don't you go direct the response?" I said.

Julio nodded and headed back to the curb to make sure that no one tried to pull into the lot or come across the lawn. You couldn't assume that, just because the area was draped with four-inch-wide, bright yellow crime scene tape, people wouldn't go over it or under it. Hell, sometimes it was our own responders who were the worst offenders.

I kneeled down beside Cara. "Did you recognize the body?"

"No, but I couldn't see his face very well. He was lying on his stomach. It's not anyone who works here."

She was trembling a little and I put my hand on her knee to steady her nerves. "Are you all right?"

"I think so. But… it's just such a shock."

"Did you see anyone leave the building when you came up? Or loitering outside?"

"No, and I would have 'cause there's never anyone around before eight. I'm sure I'd have noticed."

"Was the alarm on when you got here?"

"Funny... Now that you mention it, I know that I went in and pushed the buttons on the alarm, but I don't think it was on. Larry, I really need to get back in there to check on all the animals and start walking the dogs," she said, referring to the clinic's regular overnight collection of boarders and animals recovering from surgeries or illness.

"I'm sorry, but they'll have to wait a little longer."

"But we've got two cats who need medicine and a Bassett that's sick..." Her voice was becoming shrill with anxiety. I took her by the shoulders and stopped her.

"Cara, look at me. It's going to be okay. I promise you, as soon as Shantel and Marcus get here, I'll go through the back with you so you can check on all the animals. Okay?"

I pulled her to me and gave her a hug. I could feel her shaking, almost hyperventilating, but as I held her she regained control. She sniffed a couple of times and then sat back up.

"I'm better. I just need to make sure they're all okay."

I saw the crime scene van roll up to the curb. "They're here. It'll be just a few more minutes. Did you notice anything else out of place? Was the door locked?"

"I don't know. I just put my key in the door like normal and turned it. I didn't try the door first. I didn't notice anything, but I went in the front door and never got past the first hallway."

"Do you always go in the front door?"

"The light switches for most of the building are in that first hallway, so it's just the most convenient way to go. And all of the notes and charts for the animals in recovery are on the door. That way I can check them and know what to expect before opening the door and getting them all excited."

"Were the lights on or off?"

"Off. I'm pretty sure about that."

Cara seemed to be focusing better. Questioning a witness can sometimes calm them down. But memory is a funny thing and you don't always get the best information from a witness right away. At first, their mind remembers events through the tunnel vision of adrenaline. But, given time, their brain will remember the experience more like it actually happened and less how their pumped-up nerves experienced events. Of course, it helps if their memory is allowed to recover organically over a couple of days without being influenced by outside information.

Leaving Cara, I went over and explained the situation to Shantel Williams and Marcus Brown, our two best crime scene techs. They made quick work of their examination of the back of the clinic, and within half an hour Cara and a kennel tech who had just shown up were taking care of the animals in the boarding area.

From all appearances, neither the victim nor the killer had entered the area where the animals were. The back door had been locked and the windows were intact and secured with iron bars on the outside. Veterinary clinics, like doctors' offices, are often targeted by addicts looking for drugs, so most of them have decent security. I had high hopes that we'd be able to use that fact to make quick work of this case. I thought it was possible that a couple of addicts had broken in and gotten into a fight, resulting in one of them lying on the floor in a pool of his own blood. It wouldn't be the first time that a falling out between crooks had resulted in a murder.

My partner, Darlene Marks, called to check in with me. I told her to take her time getting to the scene. Everything was under control and it would be a little while before we'd have a chance to get in and look at the body. As I hung up, the van from the coroner's office drove up. I gave Dr. Darzi's assistants the same speech and we settled in to wait on Shantel and Marcus.

Thirty minutes later, having finished with their photos and video of the entire scene, they gave us the high sign. Darlene arrived just before we reached the clinic's front door.

Inside, everything looked normal, as far as I could tell. We went past reception, through a door and into the hallway where we could see a body splayed out on the floor. I moved closer, looking for anything—a footprint, a smudge on the wall, a dropped pencil. But all I saw was a white male dressed in cargo pants and a polo shirt, lying in a small puddle of blood. Had he been stabbed? Shot? Clearly the blood was coming from his front side as there were no exit wounds on his back.

I leaned down and tried to get a look at his face. Adams County was small and anyone working in law enforcement quickly learned the identities of most of our bad guys. Half the time, if you didn't know them, then you at least knew their family. But looking at the guy laid out on the floor, I got nothing. He appeared to be in his thirties and had blond hair. His face looked good—no obvious signs of drug use. Meth addicts were the worst. But this guy seemed pretty healthy. Except, of course, for the fact that he was dead.

"We know this guy?" Darlene asked, moving closer and peering at him.

"I don't think I've seen him before. I was just getting ready to look for a wallet."

I patted down his back pockets. Nothing. I could just reach his front one and managed to hit pay dirt, pulling out a nylon wallet. I found a Georgia driver's license for one John C. Rybeck. The picture on the license was a match for our corpse. I showed it to Darlene.

"Address up in Columbus. Look at the clothes. Could be military or ex-military," Darlene suggested.

Cargo pants and surplus boots weren't that unusual, but coupled with an address in a military town like Columbus, it gave us a big maybe. Fort Benning accounted for a lot of guys between twenty and forty in the Columbus area.

According to the victim's license, he was thirty-two years old.

"No military ID," I said, flipping through the wallet and finding only credit cards and insurance cards. There was also about a hundred bucks in cash.

Dr. Darzi's people had been watching us patiently. "All yours," I told them as Darlene and I stepped back.

After they'd taken the body's temperature and wrapped the hands and boots in bags to preserve trace evidence, they carefully turned the body over.

"Wow!" Darlene said.

"Didn't see that coming," I said, equally surprised. The blood that had pooled around him and soaked the front of his shirt came from a blood bag crushed underneath him. Stuck in his chest was the needle of a large syringe. I called Marcus back over to take more pictures. We were worried that moving the body, no matter how carefully, would dislodge it.

"I think we should remove the needle," suggested one of Darzi's assistants. "If we put him in a body bag, we're liable to pull it out or bend it. We'd risk losing any of the liquid that's still in the body or the needle of the syringe."

"Agreed," I said. "And you'd better take the blood bag for testing too."

Both of them nodded and went about their business as professionally as a dead body would allow them. I'd seen some pretty awkward dances with corpses over the years as some resisted all efforts to be put in a body bag.

"I've got a question. Why leave the wallet?" I asked Darlene as we stood by and watched the guys work. Other than the wallet, the rest of his pockets had been empty. No keys and no phone. "I understand the killer taking the cell phone—it could have incriminating texts or messages on it. Also the keys. Maybe they came in the same car. But why leave his wallet?"

"I'll take 'Criminals Are Stupid' for 500, Alex."

"There's always that," I agreed. "We can subpoena John

Rybeck's phone records and get most of the information that's on the phone."

"Unless he had a burner phone."

"That's possible. But this guy looks like he should have his own phone too."

"It's early days," Darlene said with a little smile. "You can go out and see about your girlfriend if you want. I'll finish up in here."

ACKNOWLEDGMENTS

Thanks to everyone who has read and enjoyed this series so far—I am humbled by how well it has done and I'm glad that others seem to enjoy reading this series as much as I enjoy writing it.

As always, I have to recognize the amazing and constant support and encouragement I've received from H. Y. Hanna, as well as her original cover design. Words cannot express my appreciation for all her help.

If you can have one thing in life, choose luck. I was very lucky indeed to have met a woman who could be my friend, my editor and my wife. Much of what I've accomplished, including this series, could not have been done without Melanie.

Original Cover Concept by H. Y. Hanna
Cover Design by Robin Ludwig Design Inc.
www.gobookcoverdesign.com

ABOUT THE AUTHOR

A. E. Howe lives and writes on a farm in the wilds of north Florida with his wife, horses and more cats than he can count. He received a degree in English Education from the University of Georgia and is a produced screenwriter and playwright. His first published book was *Broken State*; the Larry Macklin Mysteries is his first series and he has plans for more. Howe is also the co-host of the "Guns of Hollywood" podcast, part of the Firearms Radio Network. When not writing or podcasting, Howe enjoys riding, competitive shooting and working on the farm.

Made in United States
North Haven, CT
17 February 2024

48835594R00139